The Chronicles of Krystonia

Translated by
BEAU DIX
and
MARK SCOTT

Published by Mildonian Ltd., T/A Panton Int.

Text Copyright Beau Dix © April, 1987

Illustrations Copyright Mark Newman © April, 1987

Set in 12/13pt Baskerville
Typeset by Facsimile Typesetters Ltd., Kendal, Cumbria, England.
Printed by Frank Peters Colour Printers, Kendal, Cumbria, England.

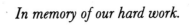

In memory of our hard work.

"On second thought, I think I might stay a while longer."

Moplos.
'The Chronicles of Krystonia.'

Author's Note

We have exhausted the combined resources of the libraries of Oxford University, Cambridge University and the three books at Keele University for our translation of the Krystonian Parchments. The translation has required certain literary licence: i.e. 'A day is a day,' 'Snow is snow,' and a Hagga-Beast is absolutely terrible.

Beau Dix and Mark Scott
April, 1987.

KRYSTONIA

I am Kephren, the recorder of the tales of the past and the deeds of the present.

Age has brought a stiffness to my joints which prevents me wandering any great distance from my home here in the Forest of Keldorran. In weather such as this it is better that I throw another log on the fire, draw up my chair close to its warmth, and continue with my work — snow is best enjoyed from the comfort of a fireside when you reach my age. Thankfully, my home in the hollow trunk of an ancient keldorr tree has stood firm against the winds of far more winters than I have seen or am ever likely to see; it may creak and groan in protest, but its door and shutters fit tightly in their frames and do not permit the slightest draught to flicker the candle flame by which I write. I can sit here, snug and secure, whilst outside the blizzard sweeps down from the Mountains of Kappah, through Keldorran and into the Valley of Wendlock.

I have not always led such a sedentary existence as now. In my youth I was forever drawn by the uncertainty and excitement which, I felt, awaited me beyond each and every horizon. Then I had known no real home, for home was wherever I happened to be when the sun set and, though many were the times on cold nights when I had dreamt of a warm bed, there was always the thought of what the morrow might bring. Though I had not realised it at the time, those days were truly beyond price. It was then that I learned many languages and customs of the inhabitants of Krystonia, and developed an ability with words that would, in later life, endow me with some skill of the pen. So when the Council of Wizards decided that the time had come for everything known of Krystonia — its history, lore and ongoing tide of events — to be documented in a single hand, I was summoned and readily agreed to such an undertaking.

Though it is proving no simple task, it allows me to enjoy

many of those things which provide comfort in old age: a permanent home, good friends and a worthy sense of purpose.

When the night sky is clear and the shutters are thrown open, I can sit in my chair and look far beyond the forest into the distance, where the Mountains of Kappah reach aloft like grim giants with their heads often lost in the clouds. As night falls I frequently watch the moons, Gos and Ghedra, appear from behind the mountains, one after the other, on a journey traversing the length of Krystonia.

Many of the older manuscripts tell of a time when Gos travelled alone. I cannot say whether this is truth or legend as the manuscripts relate that they are themselves only translations of an account to be found in a book of extreme antiquity. If such a book exists, if indeed it ever did, I should dearly love to possess it for even a short while, to extrapolate from the roots of legend a new reality. I do not open those manuscripts frequently, for their yellowed parchments are brittle and cracked with age, and I fear they might fall to dust in my hands. Yet I recall the words of the oldest as clearly as though they were now before me . . .

'There was a time with a single moon in the sky, and the lands upon which its light fell were of a beauty without equal. Above these lands flew the birds of the air, borne upon fair winds, who brought music to those who dwelt below. The birds are no longer and the names of those who heard them are lost. We know them only as The Ancients.

For there came from the darkness a new star. And in its passing the second moon came to keep company with the first. The shadow of the second moon called the seas to rise up and cover the lowlands and caused the very mountains to

"I am Kephren, Recorder of the Tales."

crack and tremble and issue forth with fire and thunder. It was from their furnaces that the shining stones came to be.

Then came the dark coldness in which all the voices were silenced . . .

It was some time before I unravelled the message contained within that passage but, fortunately, several later manuscripts held direct translations of single lines or words whose meaning might otherwise have eluded me. Piece by piece my own version was compiled and entered into these books which I now write, that it may be read long after the words of the old manuscript have faded completely.

There was never any doubt in my mind that the 'shining stones' to which it refers could be anything other than the Krystals — the stones of power. On those occasions when my eyes have grown tired and my hands unsteady with the fatigue of work, I have removed such a Krystal from a box of dark korfa wood next to my inkwell and watched as the candle flame activated the Krystal's power and caused it to burst forth with Fired-Light. Then my eyesight has sharpened and my exhaustion has been supplanted by new vigour.

Yes, the Krystals. Without these mysterious stones, life in Krystonia would be one of little comfort. Ours would be a land without seasons — a land of perpetual snow and ice. Only with the Krystals can those who are versed in weather-lore banish the cold of winter and usher in the seasons of Reawakening, Growth and Harvest. They must be forever diligent in their efforts, for there is one who desires to undo all of their good and force Krystonia to embrace everlasting winter . . . N'Borg. You will learn of him later.

Prominent in the lives of many Krystonians is the never-ending search for new Krystals, to replace those whose powers have been exhausted. It is their power which makes them so essential to spellworkers for, when incantations are woven through Krystals, whether good or evil in intent, the effect is magnified greatly. Care must always be exercised in their use, for even the simple Charm-words of the most inept apprentice, when whispered through a Krystal, can engender a spell beyond the greatest Master Wizard's ability to contain. All Krystals found are passed on to the wizards, for they are not easily obtained and their power must not be squandered but used wisely for the common good.

Not everyone who belongs to the Council of Wizards weaves spells. Rueggan, for one, has the title of wizard but, as far as I am aware, has never spoken a single incantation. His talent lies in making machines rather than magic. In his workshop, deep within a cavern in the Valley of Wendlock, he employs Krystals to instill new life into the dead machines of The Ancients, so that they may lighten the workload of us all.

Nothing gives Rueggan more satisfaction than to see one of his inventions help to make life easier for a friend. It is thanks to him that I no longer need call upon a Krystal's powers to restore my failing eyesight quite so often as before. He uncovered the secret of a hard and transparent mineral which makes all things seem sharper when seen through. Now, with the aid of a pair of highly polished chips, set into a frame which sits lightly upon my nose, I am able to decipher the faintest words in the poorest light.

There have, however, been several instances when Rueggan's creations have not behaved according to his expectations. He never fails to take these setbacks in his stride, usually dismissing them with a nonchalant wave of his hand as he mutters, "Oh well, back to the drawing board," or, "it just needs a few minor adjustments." I can testify, from personal experience, that one in particular required major alterations indeed. I remember the incident with extreme clarity . . .

I was lying upon my bed, stealing a few extra moments of sleep after working long into the previous night, when sounds of furtive scraping outside my shuttered window woke me up. Reluctantly raising my weary body, I donned my tunic and shuffled across to investigate. As I drew back the door's wooden bolt, the noises ceased abruptly.

I opened the door and the darkness of my room was suddenly flooded with early morning sunlight, causing me to squint and shield my eyes from the unaccustomed brightness. There before me, clearly exhausted, were three Gorphs, slumped against an extremely large sack to which they had all been tied.

I should explain that Gorphs are short, pudgy little brown creatures with very big eyes, seemingly assembled in a loose variety of amorphous furry lumps. Why Rueggan should even attempt to train them as assistants has long since baffled me. It was with some irritation that I enquired of them his whereabouts.

One of the Gorphs stirred and wearily nudged another who, in turn, reached over and poked the third Gorph in the ear. On letting out a squeak of surprise it stood up, attempted to assume an air of authority and, with a flourish of its chubby arm, pointed out a piece of parchment attached to the top of the sack. Its duty duly discharged, the Gorph collapsed upon its companions who seemed too tired to care.

I picked up the parchment upon which, partially obscured by greasy thumb-prints, was written in Rueggan's hand:

'DEAR FRIEND. PLEASE FIND ENCLOSED
ONE MACHINE TO TENDERISE TOUGH
FOOD. I KNOW IT WILL BE OF THE

UTMOST VALUE TO YOU. HAVE A GOOD
BREAKFAST!
RUEGGAN.

NEARLY FORGOT. HAVE BEEN CALLED
AWAY TO SHEPF'S TOWER TO FIX
WINDMILL. PLEASE LOOK AFTER GORPHS.
BE BACK SOON.

The Gorphs regarded me expectantly. Folding the note
with a sigh, I suggested they might as well take up their
burden and carry it inside. They compliantly hoisted the
sack and, with much straining and grunting, staggered
through the doorway to the centre of my room, whereupon
they let it fall with a resounding thump. I placed
Rueggan's note upon my work-table and turned to face
them. I could see only two.

From under the sack came a muffled squeal that grew
louder and more strident. Realising their companion's
misfortune, the two visible Gorphs scuttled around to the
other side where a small foot was protruding. Only with
my assistance did they manage to lift the sack high enough
to allow the trapped Gorph to escape. It lay in a pique on
the floor, ruffled and scruffed, glaring at its companions. I
really abhorr such clutter and disorder. Oh well . . .

After helping the prostrate Gorph to its feet and making
sure it was none the worse for wear, I considered what
should be done with my three unexpected charges. "You
fellows hungry?" I asked.

They nodded eagerly.

I removed from my pantry a bowl of ripe berries which I
placed on the floor before them. Their attentions now
occupied with breakfast, I set about preparing my own.

I was about to take down a pot of honey from a shelf in
the pantry when I noticed a basket full of juber-root, my

favourite staple, stored there since last harvest. Though tasty enough when stewed, it tastes even better when raw; its chewing, however, requires strong teeth which I no longer possess. Then I remembered Rueggan's machine. Perhaps now I could eat the juber in the manner I preferred.

I hurried back into the room and began untying the sack. The Gorphs looked on with mild interest, their mouths stuffed with berries and juice running down their chins. The sacking slipped away to reveal a silvery contraption, roughly oblong and standing on four stumpy legs. At the front was a hatch which, when lifted, exposed what looked suspiciously like rows of teeth. Taking a generous helping of the root, I tossed it into this cavity and closed the hatch.

For a while nothing happened and then, almost imperceptibly, the machine began to shudder and emit a low growl. I stood back as, moment by moment, the shudders became more violent and the growl developed into a thunderous roar.

As I looked on in bewilderment, the three Gorphs abandoned their berries and clutched one another in terror. They have, you understand, seen the end result of many of Rueggan's experiments. Simultaneously they croaked, "Yeak!" "Yurk!" and "Oh — Oh!"

Suddenly the noise stopped and the machine stood perfectly still. While the Gorphs maintained their grip on each other, I leaned forward expectantly and made to open the hatch.

At the very instant my fingers came in contact with the machine, it sprang sideways, landed on the hearth-rug and let out a bellicose growl. I leaped backward in alarm, tripped over the Gorphs' breakfast and fell to the floor — my impact cushioned by the winded Gorphs.

Many of my manuscripts were dislodged from their

shelves in the ensuing confusion and plummeted down on the Gorphs and myself. Fighting clear of the tangle of limbs and parchment, I glanced at the machine. It had crawled off the hearth-rug and was sidling towards me, still growling with menacing intent.

My fellow mortals scattered, diving for whatever cover was nearest. One jumped into a stewing pot, another shot under the bed, while the third leapt into an empty chest and dropped the lid down tight.

I snatched up a heavy wooden ladle and stepped towards the machine. It took a step towards me. I stepped back. The machine took another step towards me! I jumped backwards and came up against the unyielding wall of my tree. Assessing the situation, I saw just one course of action left. Taking a deep breath, I lunged forward and smacked the machine a smart blow. It must have been surprised, for it retreated a short distance. Determined to press home my advantage, I went on the offensive, brandishing my weapon.

The upshot of two vigorous circuits of my room was utter chaos. Closing my eyes to the tooth-marked furniture and to the thoroughly chewed ladle in my hand, I managed to entice the machine towards the open pantry; needing no second chance I kicked it inside and quickly slammed the door.

Time and again the machine hurled itself frantically against the inside of the door. Then, presumably sensing that its prison was well stocked with food, it turned its attention within, gobbling, crunching and gnashing its way through the shelves, keldorr wood and all. I tried to imagine the sorry state my larder must be in although, compared to the horrors of confronting that awful machine, it seemed a very small price to pay!

One by one, the Gorphs emerged from hiding and set about exploring the contents of my room as though nothing had happened. (Their attention spans are notoriously short.)

"Make yourself useful and help me tidy up," I said to the Gorph which always seemed to act as spokesman for the group; it stared at me innocently as though not comprehending. "Or else . . . !" I barked, leaving my threat unfinished whilst pointing to the pantry door. Instant comprehension!

All three immediately made a great show of being helpful; but, I quickly recalled, no matter how obliging Gorphs may appear to be, they never provide the kind of assistance which leads to order and calm. No sooner had I reprimanded one of them for depositing my writing quills in the honey jar, than I had to dash across the room to where another was gleefully stacking my manuscripts in the wash basin.

"Stop!" I said loudly. Determined not to suffer any further chaos, I stomped towards the Gorphs who cowered on my approach. "Sit in that corner," I directed. "Go on!"

The Gorphs looked up at me with pained expressions and then at one another before trudging hand-in-hand into the corner. Any pangs of guilt I may have felt about treating such well-meaning beasts in this way were soon dispelled by the sight of my sodden parchments floating in the basin.

I righted the furniture, restored my scattered quills to their usual pot and took the wet parchments outside to dry. It was such a fine and pleasant morning that I longed to relax and recuperate in the sun for a while. But, not daring to leave my charges unattended for any length of time, I hastened back inside. Deciding to take what advantage I could of the weather, I grabbed a hooked pole and opened the shutters set high in the walls of my home. Sunlight poured through, illuminating the whole interior.

I sat at my table and placed a clean sheet of parchment

before me, intending to log some notes which would later be useful when I came to set down my account of the day's events. But, no sooner had I dipped my quill into the inkwell than the shaft of golden light which bathed my desk flickered and disappeared.

I looked up, expecting to see a dark cloud obscuring the sun, when the whole of the room seemed to erupt in a frantic whirring of wings. "Owheeeey!" came a cry, followed by a dull thud as something collided with the side of a cupboard, upset more of my parchments, flopped headlong onto my table, rolled off and dropped unceremoniously to the floor with a painful "Ouch!"

I peered over the table's edge as a dishevelled tangle of flesh unwound into the shape of a small dragon. "Owhey!" I exclaimed.

The dragon stared at me apologetically. "S . . . S . . . Sorry," he stuttered. "Wings not work right yet."

What Owhey lacked in his mastery of flight he more than made up with his talent for causing a nuisance. Three Gorphs, a homicidal machine, and an Inexperienced Flying Object all in the span of one morning. Not only in one morning, but in one house. My house! It surely looked to be one of 'those days'. "Who's with you?" I asked.

Owhey shook his head.

"Nobody? Then what are you doing so far from home?"

"Lost," he replied, adding thoughtfully, "Wrong turn at Wendlock." He flapped his wings vigorously with determined concentration and began to rise till he hovered at the height of my table-top. The turbulence thus stirred sent my parchments spiralling madly into the air.

"No," I protested. "Stop!"

Owhey descended obediently, but too quickly. "Ouch!" he groaned, bouncing upon the floor. "Fly good when big," he assured me.

"No doubt you will. But flying is for the great outdoors; not inside my home!"

"Home? Good idea! Owhey want to go home!" He regarded me with his large doleful eyes, before attempting again to get himself airborne.

Deciding it would be in both our interests to prevent any more disturbance, I secured Owhey to the leg of my table by means of a stout length of twine. "Sit quietly," I patted his head reassuringly. "I'll have someone come by to collect you."

I picked up my prized Phargol-horn and, stepping outside, pressed it to my lips and blew hard. With the horn, a gift from the Council of Wizards, I could summon anyone within earshot to run errands for me as required. Its booming monotone reverberated through the forest and I wondered who would respond.

"Hear that, Owhey?" I asked, returning to my table. "Someone will come for you soon . . . I hope!"

Again I set out a clean sheet of parchment and began to write industriously, striving to make up for lost time. As I worked, Owhey nodded off and slept contentedly at my feet. The Gorphs too, no doubt tired by their earlier exertions, snored rhythmically, huddled together in the corner. Only the sound of Rueggan's machine, apparently suffering from an attack of indigestion, disturbed the peace with intermittent loud burps. I had almost begun to believe that life had returned to normal when the tranquility of the long afternoon was shattered by a piercing wail which grew louder as it came near.

"Spyke!" exclaimed Owhey, suddenly wide awake.

Spyke was an adolescent dragon who liked singing. In fact he adored singing. Singing was what he lived for. Unfortunately, what he could do to a song was not far short of a criminal act. My shoulders sagged at the mention of his name.

"Hi there, Keph old buddy!" he greeted me, his bulk filling the doorway and casting a long shadow into my room. (Even adolescent dragons are large.) "Heard your horn, Keph. Know what? It kinda' inspired me."

"Oh no," I muttered, knowing too well what was coming next.

"Sorry Keph. Can you say that again?"

"I said that's wonderful. Now why don't you take off with Owhey and commit it to parchment some place else?"

"Dragons can't write, Keph. You know that."

"Nor can they sing," I mumbled.

"I thought I'd let ya hear it," he gushed, "before I forget the tune."

"Good idea," I snapped; "to forget it, I mean!"

"Just the first verse," he pressed. "You'll love it!" He took a deep breath, preparing to inflict his song upon me and my uninvited guests.

"Not today," I hissed through clenched teeth, holding up my hand. "I'm far too busy. Hurry along and take Owhey. He's going to be late for his dinner."

"Okay . . . How about just the opening line? It's the best I've composed yet."

"No! Not even a single note!"

"It goes something like this . . ."

"No!" I hastily untied Owhey as Spyke was filling his lungs. When he opened his mouth to burst forth, I thrust the rope between his teeth and gagged him, just in time. He gulped and looked offended, having finally got the message. Snorting derisively, he stomped away, towing young Owhey behind him.

Afternoon gave way to a cool calm evening. By then the food-machine, having digested the entire foodstock and fittings of my pantry and overcome its bout of indigestion, had begun gnawing furiously at the bottom of the door. It would almost certainly have escaped and resumed our earlier battle, had not Rueggan arrived when he did. As it was, it took the concerted efforts of myself, the wizard and the three Gorphs to overpower the machine and marshal it back in the sack. Without the smallest apology, Rueggan vanished into the forest, followed by the Gorphs and his gluttonous food machine.

I spent a restless night being constantly disturbed by a rumbling sound, just like a low angry growl. Several times I sat up with a start, sure the machine had turned to exact a terrible revenge. I was more than a little relieved to discover that the cause of the noise was none other than my stomach, protesting its own deprivation and hunger.

Next morning, at first light, the Gorphs returned to my home with supplies from Rueggan to replenish my larder. This time, I did not let them anywhere near the threshold!

The dragons present something of a mystery. Whilst the ancestral line of almost all Krystonians can be traced back in time through the oldest manuscripts, no mention is made of dragons till somewhat later. Many times have I tried and failed to discover a satisfactory explanation. The dragons have been of little help as they themselves do not keep written records. Yet, no account of Krystonia could be considered complete without describing their contribution.

Where the snow-covered Mountains of Kappah meet the forbidding Waste of Shugg, stand three imposing peaks of naked rock. At this junction of Krystonia's two great mountain ranges, the ground is heated by subterranean fires that smoulder interminably far below. Snowfall is quickly melted, evaporating in thick, billowing clouds of steam and vapour. In the caverns which honeycomb the largest peak, Cairn Tor, live the dragons — for only here can they find sufficient warmth to survive the harsh winters and incubate their eggs. It is from Cairn Tor that their business endeavors are directed by their elected leader, the Grumblypeg dragon, Grunch.

Like all Grumblypeg dragons, Grunch is quite large and, having no wings, cannot fly. Leadership apart, he is perhaps best known for his disposition. He never laughs nor smiles; he just grumbles . . . always! If the sun shines, he insists it is too hot; if it rains, then it is too wet. If it does neither he complains that the weather is too unpredictable. Yet, surprising as it may seem, he is not unpopular. On the contrary, he is respected as being thoroughly trustworthy and completely dependable, and has ensured that the dragons live in comfort whilst the needs of their clients are always satisfied.

When Gurneyfoot, the oldest dragon, was forced by failing memory and ill-health to retire, he handed over control of a modest business, maintained at a level sufficiently intensive to excuse himself and other males from the tedious chore of egg-sitting. Upon his retirement, Grunch was elected leader, assuming responsibilities for overseeing all business interests which related to the dragons. Grunch, unlike Gurneyfoot and any dragon before, had mastered a skill which would stand him in good stead — he had taught himself to read. He has since, as a matter of interest, made it standard policy that all young dragons be taught.

There exists a series of treaties and compacts between the dragons and other Krystonians whereby the former provide aerial and ground transportation in return for provisions of the charcoal and grain mixture which they require for sustenance and as fuel for stoking their internal boilers.

In Grunch's opinion, the contracts in force when he succeeded Gurneyfoot were too favourable to the client. However, not being the sort to break a bond once made, he ensured that all obligations were met until the agreements expired at the end of the Season of Growth. Only then did Grunch act, flatly refusing to further implement the treaties until they had been renegotiated. Protest as they might, other Krystonians could not move him to accept a single grain or lump of charcoal less than for what he held out. Eventually, with the busy Season of Harvest already well underway, the client's negotiators relented and signed the new terms.

But it could never be said that Grunch had held them to ransom. The new rates of compensation were truly fair, and any grumblings that persisted after the signing were, predictably, Grunch's own. Perhaps it was this early success that led him to become rather complacent and to make a deal that still irks him to this day.

A Master-Wizard whose name is Graffyn has the

responsibility of testing the reliability and effectiveness of all spells before they can be accepted by the Council of Wizards. He is also, by all accounts, the only person to have ever succeeded in getting the better of Grunch in a business arrangement. I mention it here to explain how the partnership, which still persists between Graffyn and the Grumblypeg dragon, first came into existence. The episode was related to me by the wizard himself, when I happened to question him why he seemed to experience no difficulty in getting the leader of Dragon Transport Limited to ferry him about — a privilege which Grunch extends to no other. In the interest of presenting a balanced account, I did invite Grunch to contribute his version, but he became rather irate and, grumbling as ever, stomped off.

The account runs as follows . . .

Early one morning, before the dawn, Graffyn approached Grunch in an effort to secure transport to various locations for the evaluation of some particular spells. After complaining profusely about the timing of his call, Grunch listened to Graffyn's requirements before offering him use of the winged dragon, Groosh.

"Ah. There's a problem, you see," Graffyn explained. "Not only is Groosh's motto 'Direct flight — No layovers' but I cannot bear heights. They make me positively ill."

"Then tell him to fly low," Grunch rumbled testily.

"That will not do at all," replied Graffyn. "No matter how low it seems to him, it will still be too high for me. Whatever I sit upon must remain in contact with the ground at all times."

"Can't be done," Grunch argued. "All Grumblypegs are fully booked."

"It must be done," insisted Graffyn. "This work is vital to the Council of Wizards!"

"They should have appointed someone who doesn't get

airsick," Grunch retorted in admonishment. "There is nothing I can do to help you."

"Why can't you take me?" asked Graffyn.

Grunch was incredulous. "What? Me? I have far too many other things to do ... Dragon Transport Limited does not run by itself. Why, I have schedules to check, I have to make sure that the paperwork ... Oh, forget it! What do wizards know about business anyway?"

"Quite a lot as a matter of fact. 'Business first — Customer second'; isn't that the first principle of success?"

Grunch's eyes opened wide. "Absurd! That's what I mean; wizards know nothing about business. What you describe is a recipe for disaster. The customer always comes first!"

"Always?" queried Graffyn. "Always?"

"Always," reiterated Grunch. "The customer always comes first! Now why don't you go and ..."

"But surely," injected Graffyn, "there must be some exceptions?"

"No. No exceptions," Grunch replied. "The customer always comes ..." Realising his mistake, he fixed Graffyn with a vexed stare and growled, "where to, when and for how long?"

"Wherever, whenever and for however long it takes," said Graffyn, smiling pleasantly.

"Won't be cheap," Grunch replied, groping for a chance to redeem the situation without losing face.

"That's alright," Graffyn said airily. "Bill The Council."

Grunch's comprehensive approach to matters pertaining to the transport business does not reflect the feelings of all male dragons. Many merely see it as a way of escaping mundane tasks around the caverns; a few prefer to brood eggs and clean the caves while their mates go out on errands. Grunch, being a chauvinist, tries to discourage this by claiming that females are not strong enough to carry viable loads. Many customers, on the contrary, prefer to travel by female dragons, regarding them as less likely to engage in impromptu aerobatics than the more impulsive males. This concern is, at times, well justified, as what happened on Spyke's inaugural flight with a client on board will amply serve to illustrate.

Spyke favoured his passenger with a half-day's medley of songs, confusing the slaps and kicks he received as signs of appreciation. Taking things a step further, he introduced the fellow to high-altitude stalls, vertical crash dives, tree-top recoveries and loop-the-loops. There was no reaction by then from the rider, interpreted by Spyke as sheer enthralment with his skills. Only after landing and the reins were cut from the poor customer's hands, did it become clear that he was in a state of catatonic shock!

Though Spyke is less profit-oriented than Grunch, he does at least show concern for the business. Others have no interest in its workings whatsoever. The Grumblypeg, Stoope is such an example, devoting most of his energies to a passion for entertaining, notably in the form of oft-rehearsed, but rarely successful, exhibitions of colour-co-ordinated flamethrowing and magic under the title of 'STOOPE THE STOOPENDOUS — THE ONE DRAGON SHOW'.

The attention-seeking Stoope is forever attempting to corral spectators for his shows. The adults, having seen his limited repertoire many times before, generally decline. But the younger dragons eagerly await his performances.

Among the audience at one particular show was Grall, a silent and stony winged adolescent who had developed a reputation for petty cruelty and unprovoked malevolence. He was seated at the back of the crowd as Stoope launched into his well-worn presentation.

"Welcome everyone, young and old, to my little show. You are about to see things that will astound you and amaze, things that will baffle and bewilder." The young dragons murmured with anticipation as they settled in for the performance while Grall looked on with bored disdain, determined to remain unimpressed.

"To begin with," went on Stoope, "I will endeavour to divert you with a few tricks of fire. I shall produce from my mouth flames of every colour imaginable. I must, at this juncture, remind the youngsters among us that these tricks should only be attempted by an expert," adding vainly, ". . . like myself."

Stoope then commenced with a clever and inspired display, spanning the entire spectrum. The young dragons gleefully slapped their tails as each new flame was spectacularly produced. Grall still showed no reaction.

At the end of the fire-breathing element of his act, Stoope bowed low, basking in the adulation. He did not notice the low grunts of derision that came from Grall.

"Thank you, my friends," Stoope continued, raising high his paws, waiting for the silence which quickly descended. "And now, a very special trick taught to me by The Great Gadzoot, a travelling magician of famed renown; disappearance!"

'Oohs' and 'Aahs' of anticipation greeted his announcement.

"This particular trick requires a certain amount of audience participation, without which the magic will not work. Would you all, please, close your eyes."

The youngsters obeyed, covering their eyes and giggling as they did so.

"All eyes shut tight?" Stoope asked as he sidled towards a large boulder. Then, with a quick sidelong glance to check he was not being observed, he ducked smartly out of sight, curling his long tail beneath him. "No peeking! When I count to three, open your eyes and you will see me no more, for I will then have . . . vanished!" He tittered to

The Gorphs prepare themselves as Rueggan begins another experiment.

himself. This was his favourite part of the show. "One . . . two . . . three!"

The young dragons' eyes shot open to gasps of amazement.

"I am invisible!" Stoope proclaimed.

The crowd had started to applaud when a voice at the back called out: "He's behind that rock!" It belonged to Grall.

"I am not behind any rock, young dragons. I have, in fact, disappeared."

"I saw him do it," heckled Grall. "It's a bloody rip-off!"

"No! No," Stoope gritted his teeth. "You're much mistaken there."

Grall rose and made to approach Stoope's hiding place when Flayla, a female acting as the youngsters' nanny, intercepted him in two earth-trembling strides. She towered over the adolescent, blue smoke wisping from her nostrils as anger stoked her flame-pressure. Grall could feel the heat of her breath as she hissed slowly, "Don't steal away the dreams of the young."

Grall gazed into her reddening eyes and realised that he had met his match. Flayla's size and threatening bulk, and her low throat-rumbling which swelled increasingly loud, made argument futile. Not prepared to risk the embarrassment of a scorching, he walked slowly away.

In the few moments that the audience's attention had been drawn to this unexpected sideshow, Stoope seized upon the opportunity to save his credibility and darted from behind the boulder, effecting a miraculous reappearance.

"Rock? Rock! Did somebody say rock?" he laughed as all eyes returned upon him. "Now I must go and rest; disappearance is a particularly exhausting trick." In response to his audience's cheers, Stoope gave a low and dignified bow. "And in my next show," he grandly proclaimed, "I shall introduce you to my amazing bottomless bag of mind-boggling tricks!"

That episode marked the beginning of an ever-widening gulf between Grall and the rest of dragon society. He took by force that which he could not obtain by trickery and was shunned before long by all others of his kind — even those who had hatched from the same brood of eggs. Left alone to sit and scheme, he grew nastier and more sullen. He sought power over others and yet hated any who exercised power over him. As he grew into adulthood, those dragons who could prevent him from having his way with others grew fewer, till only Grunch commanded his respect — and this more by power of will than by virtue of physical strength. Now, with Grunch the only obstacle between Grall and control of Cairn Tor, it was inevitable that a confrontation would occur.

Dragons, being sociable creatures, seize any opportunity to meet in the Great Cavern and discuss day-to-day events and problems. The conclusion of these informal gatherings is marked by the departure of the females and young dragons to their caves, leaving the males to congregate in a smaller side-chamber to hear their leader's brief summary of the present state of business. After one such address, when Grunch asked for any questions, Grall stood up to speak.

"How much longer must we noble dragons suffer the indignity of being pack-animals for our inferiors?" he asked in a low even tone, carefully judging the impact of each well-chosen word on the assembly. Every dragon with the exception of Grunch, took a sharp intake of breath. All eyes centered on Grall.

"It seems clear, Grall," said Grunch, "that such a question could not have been voiced so fluently had it not been in the back of your mind for some considerable time. Perhaps there is more you would like to add?" Grunch arched one eyebrow. He knew full well there would be.

"Indeed there is," responded Grall, moving to the centre of the chamber. "Why do we who are strong, allow our lessers to dominate our lives? Why do we gratefully accept what is ours for the taking? Our skin is armoured — theirs is thin. From our mouths comes fire — from theirs hollow words of the weak. We were born to rule — not serve!" He let a tongue of flame flicker menacingly through his nostrils as his voice became louder and more threatening. "Has not the time come to strike fear in the hearts of those who view us as servants and mere conveniences? Has not the time come to take possession of what is ours by might?" He paused and added in a cajoling, sibilant whisper that reeked of malice, "To take possession of Krystonia!"

Hush fell in the cavern. Grunch rose to his feet and cleared his throat, his eyes fixed firmly on Grall. "I must thank you for such an honest and frank portrayal of your beliefs. But remember this; only because we conduct ourselves in the way we do, may you voice your opinions freely. Would such freedom exist if we followed your advice? I think not. Fear begets fear; and fear denies freedom. Any society that draws its strength from fear has room for one voice and no others. Do we, I ask you, go hungry in winter or feel the cold? No; and why? Because our friends — and they are our friends — know we cannot endure the winter unaided and so provide for us. Whilst their skin may be thinner than ours, their magic is strong. Surely magic that can control the very elements would find little difficulty in quelling the fire from our mouths? Remember, all things are in equilibrium and to upset the balance would surely see our downfall. Grall, you are still relatively young. I only hope that in time you come to know the truth in my words: we do not need to take possession of Krystonia when Krystonia already belongs to us, as it belongs to everybody. And we do exercise great influence; an influence based upon trust and friendship. And that is much stronger than fear!"

A momentary silence followed Grunch's speech, broken by a thunderous thumping of tails and cries of wholehearted agreement.

Grall glared at Grunch and began to laugh wickedly. "You fools," he mocked. "You ignorant blind fools! If my talents have no place here, I know where they will be welcomed and accorded the respect which they deserve. You shall all soon see that it is Grunch, not I, who speaks false words. I shall take pleasure in curing you of that blindness ... great pleasure!" With that, he pushed his way through the crowd, knocking aside several dragons who were slow to clear a passage.

From that time, Grall ceased to dwell in Cairn Tor. There was much speculation as to his whereabouts, followed by a wave of unconfirmed sightings. When he did finally reappear, the truth was harder to bear than the wildest rumour during his absence.

A dark shadow circling the summit of Cairn Tor, his voice echoed off the barren slopes. "Fools! Harken to the voice of N'Grall and listen well. See that I am newly named by he to whom I have sworn my allegiance; he who will surely drive you all from your caves! He who will crush all who dare oppose him! He who will rule Krystonia!"

The inhabitants of Cairn Tor looked up in consternation; the males grimly, the females protectively drawing in their young.

"See, I am all that I promised, all that you could have been had you listened to me!" He laughed, a cruel dark laugh which seemed to come from the depths of his cold unfeeling soul. "Witness the Krystal given to me by the great N'borg as a token of his favour," he sneered, the shining stone suspended from his neck on a heavy, golden chain glowing bright as though in acknowledgement of his words. "I shall never again feel the cold of winter. I shall fly free while you must huddle in your miserable caves and await the return of the warmth. Even the Mountains of Kappah cannot halt my flight! I N'Grall, mock you, revile you for what you are: servants of your own ignorance!"

He sent a sheet of crimson flame down the side of the peak as if it were a statement of his future intent. Then, laughing again, he wheeled away and arrowed in the direction of his new alliegence, turning his back on the fellowship of his own kind. N'Grall had found N'Borg; and N'Borg had found the perfect instrument for the execution of his dark designs. Many would soon bear the consequences of that evil alliance.

There is a map which hangs upon my wall. It is old and faded, and the names appear in little-known archaic script. My interest is aroused not by what the map shows, but what it omits.

The Valley of Wendlock, the Forest of Keldorran and the Shadi-Sampi Swamp are all plainly marked, as are the two great ranges of Kappah and Shugg. But east of Kappah, the ancient map is blank. At first sight, one could be forgiven for thinking that whoever sat down to draw the map had been called away before its completion, never to return. However, in extremely small lettering in the midst of this space are inscribed the words 'Uncharted Lands'.

On the map which I have begun but not, as yet, completed, many previously unknown tracts have been identified and named. Considerably more is known today of Krystonia than when the original map was lettered. And I have seen much of it for myself.

Beyond the Mountains of Kappah lies the Desert of Cluod-Hakkom, a vast, inhospitable place of only two extremes; the season of baking heat which warps the vision and deceives the eye with wild images that dance madly across the insanely shimmering horizon; and the season of anguishing cold which descends onto the Desert and bites so deep that many of the rocks and boulders disintegrate into more sand. And the wind. There is always the wind: the hot sand-scouring summer wind, and the iced bone-numbing wind of winter.

I have seen the Desert of Cluod-Hakkom and met with those who not only endure such conditions but actually thrive in them. They are the Maj-Dron.

In a land of little shelter the Maj-Dron make their own. On huge wheeled platforms called Yurda, constructed from lightweight but tough borga wood, they erect permanent tents of multi-chambers.

Throughout the two seasons the Yurda must cross a

variety of rough terrain and their wheels are of prime importance. These have evolved into peculiar affairs resembling oversized, scalloped drums. Wide, close-sided and hollow, they are also made from borga wood. Their great width and lightness disperses the weight and prevents the Yurda from sinking into sand or snow, whilst the scalloped ridges on the wheel-tracks provide extremely good purchase. The commodious tents each house at least one entire family and, in some cases, two or three. Their fabric is woven from wool, sheared from Mahoudha — the Maj-Drons' beasts of burden. So finely woven is Mahoudha wool that not even the tiniest grain of sand or smallest speck of dust penetrates the walls of the tents, which are cool and well-aired in summer and warm and wind-proof in winter.

Each Yurda is pulled by a team of Mahoudha, hairy beasts of great size and strength. Although they tower over the Maj-Dron, they are of an extremely docile nature, if somewhat disposed to being stubborn. Normally, two brace are sufficient for the task, but some Yurda are so large they necessitate three pairs in harness. Four to six Mahoudha are always tethered to the rear of each Yurda for additional power up steep inclines or brake of steep descent. The wool of the Mahoudha, sheared at winter's end and again in midsummer, not only provides material for tents but also for tunics and robes. In addition, the Mahoudha are prized for their milk, from which is made excellent butter and cheese. These gentle creatures live on a diet of the dry, scrub-thorn and fibrous grass plants that grow in the Steppe-lands; and, of course, water. Good grazing and deep drinking once every five or six days fulfils their every need.

The Maj-Dron have established a migratory pattern which circumnavigates the entire desert, travelling full circle within one cycle of the seasons. The sole time they

N'Grall tests the warming powers of the Krystal given him by N'Borg.

traverse the heart of the Cluod-Hakkom is during the yearly trek to the mining grounds. So alike do they appear in their billowing robes, their voices all of similar pitch, and their faces masked by heavy veils to protect from sand and ice storms, that only by close attention to the motif and detail of their exquisite jewelry is it possible to tell them apart. Whorls of finely spun wire from smelted ore are set with precious stones to form intricate designs, no two ever the same. Always the matrices of these designs feature particular gems that signify each individual's tribe. The source of these gemstones, known to the Maj-Dron but very few others, lies within a deep fissure called Kazm Ori.

Kazm Ori does not surrender its treasures easily. To reach the depths of this huge crevasse may take a whole day. The Maj-Dron must follow a steep and narrow path which snakes down to the mining grounds far below. The route is often blocked by rockfalls and, with the path only sufficiently wide for single file, an advance party is sent to clear the way before the main contingent follows; a single careless footfall and they may tumble into the abyss.

Those who wait to descend are faced with other dangers. The high cliffs which mark the gateway to Kazm Ori are home to the ever-watchful Kwarks. These awesome predators, gliding through the air on silent wings, can hurl down and snatch up a Maj-Dron in their hooked talons, carrying him away to their rock perches and a fate too awful to contemplate. However, only the unwary fall prey, for the Maj-Dron fend off such attacks with small slings, from which they launch rock projectiles with unerring accuracy.

Then there are the Hagga-Beast. With the maned heads and bodies of lions, huge feathered wings and the forked tails of serpents, these formidable creatures inhabit eyries jutting out from the precipitous cliff walls. Only from these high roosts can they launch themselves into the air and search for prey. They are too large to be deterred by the Maj-Drons' small weaponry and the only defence is to press tightly against a rock face which, because of their ponderous size, the Hagga cannot reach.

Once on the fissure's floor the Maj-Dron are safe from attack from the Kwarks and the Hagga, and can pitch their main encampment. The evidence of mining by countless generations is plain to see. Deep shafts gape like toothless mouths at the bottom of vertical walls, and long shafts lead into a labyrinth of subterranean galleries. Inside the caverns, flights of steps chiselled from solid rock lead to narrow, precarious walkways up which the Maj-Dron ascend to the dizzy upper levels. The light from their flaming torches flickers and dances over the marbled veins of crystalline rock, enlivening the ore with a fire of its own. Here and there a flash betrays the presence of gem stones; the red Gloris Gana, the purple Ugena Ulan and, most precious of all, the rarely-found blue Tannis Tazule.

For many days the Maj-Dron journey along the Kazm Ori, moving from one seam to the next, smelting the ore in the cool hours after darkness and just before dawn. They rest and sleep in the shade of makeshift shelters, while the sun raises the temperature between the fissure's walls to unbearably high.

Some twenty days after their descent into Kazm Ori, mining completed for another year, the Maj-Dron emerge wearily at the northernmost end and rejoin their families, their woven baskets heavy with treasure. With the Mahoudha in yoke, they break camp and strike north-west.

The Cluod-Hakkom holds treasures and surprises of many different kinds. The rages of the wind mobilise the dunes and marshall them across the desert to build others anew. What on one day lies buried may be exposed on the next and thus, in the course of their travels, the Maj-Dron often encounter new finds on unfamiliar ground. They obtain many Krystals in this fashion, which are cached safely in their tents to await a special rendezvous in the Steppes of Shimm at the foot of the Mountains of Kappah, for transfer to a representative from the Council of Wizards. They sometimes come across a machine, whole or in part, which once belonged to The Ancients. Ugly and of no value to the Maj-Dron, they are well aware of its importance to Rueggan and will go to considerable trouble to ensure that he receives it.

None know the desert so intimately as the Maj-Dron, and anyone wishing to travel the Cluod-Hakkom should do so under their guidance to stand a realistic chance of survival. I am one of only two who are known to have travelled in their company, having spent a whole year with them in my youth, as guest of their head chieftain. I taught Shigger, his heir, to read and write, out of which has developed a lasting friendship. A sizeable collection of well-written and descriptive parchments have been sent to me by Shigger in the course of many years, recording his explorations, encounters with strange and terrifying beasts, and a detailed log of the Maj-Dron migrations. It was one of Shigger's annual communications that enabled The Council of Wizards to solve a disturbing series of strange events and avert potential disaster.

A few seasons ere, a maladjustment in the normal balance of things occurred which caused the wizards great worry. Tried and tested spells failed, crops withered despite the consuming dedication of the wizardess Wodema, and unseasonable weather threatened the advent of premature winter. The Council called an emergency conclave and questioned all Apprentices, suspecting them of dabbling in incantations too advanced for their abilities. When satisfied that their pupils were not to blame, the wizards checked their own spell recipes and tested each other for errors. Still, all incantations appeared to have been conducted according to The Council's Code of Regulations. Some destructive force had obviously been unleashed but, try as they might, their now frantic investigation could not reveal the cause.

After the possible had been eliminated, the name of N'Borg, the only Master-Wizard skilled enough to create such interference and disruption with his magic, came up in passing. But N'Borg was confined to his Krak and the Waste of Shugg at all times except deepest winter. These events were happening in the temperate Season of Growth and the wizards believed his magic too weak at this time of year to cause such drastic effect.

It was then I received Shigger's yearly packet of recordings. As soon as I acquainted myself with the message contained therein, I summoned a courier with my Phargol-horn and dispatched it post-haste to the Krystellate Obelisk. The Council of Wizards read the report with alarm, for it told that a new source of evil had joined forces with N'Borg.

At the most easterly point of the Maj-Dron migration, not far from my map's 'Uncharted Lands', their oasis-encampment had been approached by a dark-cloaked figure who requested permission to accompany them westwards to the Mountains of Kappah. The Maj-Dron, not only hospitable but curious too, readily agreed. During their journey across the Cluod-Hakkom, Shigger had attempted to find out more of this stranger, being puzzled by his presence at such an unlikely location. Neither the Maj-Dron nor any other Krystonian knows what lies within the 'Uncharted Lands', and Shigger was eager to learn from whence he came. But the stranger kept himself aloof, replying to the most innocent and friendly question with a mere nod or short shake of his head. Any inquiry relating to his origin or destination, he pretended not to hear.

What Shigger did discover was by stealth. Their fellow-traveller kept a heavy-bound book about him at all times, even sleeping with it under his head. When the Maj-Dron halted for the night, he would remove himself from their camp and slink off into the sand-dunes. Shigger twice followed him unseen and perceived him reading aloud from the book in an unknown tongue, conversing with two black-winged apparitions. The stranger was undoubtedly . . . a spell-caster!

The silence which the stranger had maintained since joining the caravan, was broken the day he left the Maj-Dron and struck out alone, north-west. His departure was preceeded by a series of questions which Shigger considered ominous and which warranted mention in his dispatch.

"Are these," he had asked, "the Barren Steppes I see before me?"

Taken aback, Shigger had answered, "They are."

"Then I leave you now. Take this as payment for your services," he had said, nonchalantly tossing Shigger a small golden disc upon which some design was carved. "West of the Barren Steppes and then north lies the Waste of Shugg?"

Shigger quietly stared with an unasked but obvious question.

"Ah," the stranger knowingly responded before setting off on his own. As the figure smalled in the distance, Shigger called out after him, requesting his name.

"Chakk," he yelled over his shoulder without stopping. "You will hear it again, no doubt."

When Shigger's report was received by The Council of Wizards, along with the enclosed golden disc, the source of our problem was finally laid bare. They placed the disc beneath a Krystal and worked the incantation of Memory Of An Inanimate, charging the Krystal to reveal the identity of the disc's previous owner. A faint light blossomed and grew within; at first it broadcast a vision of Shigger.

"No, before that time," the wizard, Tador, had commanded, whereupon the image disappeared to be replaced by one of the stranger.

"His name?" Tador had asked.

"Chakk," mused a voice within the Krystal. "Now N'Chakk of the Krak N'Borg in the Waste of Shugg."

"A spell-caster?"

"Yes."

"Of what bent?"

"Of the dark," said the voice out loud.

"And of the land from whence he came?" inquired Tador.

As soon as the Krystal said, "Malforan," a confused impression of black mists drifted through the wizards minds.

"I want to see more clearly," demanded Tador.

Before the voice could respond, the Krystal's light waned and faded away. The wizards looked at each other in surprise.

"That's as much as we will learn for the moment," Tador said resignedly. "His magic must be of some power to have stifled the Krystal so quickly."

"Perhaps with help from N'Borg," mulled Haapf. The other wizards nodded in contemplative agreement.

"Well, let's get busy," said Graffyn, flicking through the pages of a book of incantations. "Ah! here's what we need . . ." Thusly did N'Chakk introduce himself. Thanks to the actions of Shigger, the Council of Wizards not only came to hear of N'Borg's latest ally but were able to quickly diffuse the effects of his dark magic.

The powers of those of the Krystellate Obelisk would yet be further taxed; of that they were forewarned.

A year went by after N'Chakk had left the Maj-Dron, before his influence was felt by them again. In the course of their migration, the caravan had lately veered from its westward route along the edge of the Barren Steppes, heading south for the Steppes of Shimm, when N'Chakk finally gave them true payment for their erstwhile hospitality. He sent N'Grall!

A black speck appeared against the sun and grew ever larger as it hurtled toward the slowly moving Yurda. To Shigger, there was something decidedly disquieting about the rapidly approaching shape. As a precaution, he ordered the caravan to form a tight defensive ring; Yurda to the outside, Maj-Dron and Mahoudha within.

The Maj-Dron were still shepherding the Mahoudha into the circle when the dragon struck. A sheet of flame issued from his mouth as he swooped from the sky, blackening the surface of the desert in its wake. The Mahoudha, feeling the searing heat and smelling the acridity of his fire, tossed their heads nervously and kicked out with their hind legs, before drawing into a tight knot to protect their calves. A second burst of flame followed close upon the first and slammed into a large Yurda. Tent and platform instantly erupted in a ball of fire, belching thick black smoke. The frightened Mahoudha trumpeted loudly and stampeded in blind panic, colliding with Yurda, knocking Maj-Dron to the ground, and raising a choking dust cloud which only increased their alarm. Spitting cinders from the burning Yurda rained down in a cascade of sparks which ignited nearby tents, whose owners beat frantically to quell the crippling flames. All the while, a dense pall of smoke spread outwards, blanketing the scene.

N'Grall circled above, gloating. He would have liked to continue his onslaught, but he had come for a specific purpose. The cloud rose and began to disperse as he spoke. "Greetings, Maj-Dron. Come forth in friendship and meet the winged N'Grall. And, as a token of your friendship, come forth with your Krystal." Descending, he laughed at his irony, his strong wings slowly beating to a hover. As the air cleared, he looked about in disbelief, for whilst he could see the still-smoking Yurda and the trembling Mahoudha, gathered some way off, there was no sign of a single Maj-Dron! "Show yourselves," he demanded.

"Go away!" a defiant voice retorted from a hidden source.

N'Grall responded by blowing a scorching flame over the heads of the Mahoudha, singeing the hairs along several backs. The shaggy beasts screamed a terrified wail in unison. "The next will find its mark," the dragon warned.

Shigger rose to his feet from out of the ground and shook off the sand from his robes. He glared at N'Grall accusingly, and then looked back at the trembling beasts. "That was a nasty thing to do," he said.

"It was hardly a sneeze compared to what I will do if you delay me further. Now do as I bid and bring out your Krystal!"

Shigger pondered, then reached into his robe, withdrew a finely-polished clear jewel-stone and stretched out his arm as though offering it to N'Grall. "Perhaps you would prefer this? . . . It has great value and many long days of hard labour have gone into cutting its facets."

"I want no trinkets," the dragon roared. "I want your Krystal! Now!"

Shigger shrugged as though in defeat, and then slightly tilted the jewel. A brilliant blinding flash of sunlight burst from the gem and exploded in N' Grall's eyes. The dragon reeled and, snarling in anger and pain, lost altitude quickly. He regained his senses just in time to avoid crashing into the ground.

Once again N'Grall rose high and once again Shigger's jewel-stone blinded him. "Enough yet dragon?"

N'Grall averted his eyes, recognising further attack to be futile. "Maj-Dron, the time will come when I return to you," he hissed. "Beware!" With a hard slap of his wings he gained more height and withdrew, heading towards the far-distant Krak N'Borg.

The Maj-Drons' southerly route along the Steppes of Shimm ends at the great Rock of Gahloth. There they turn westward, passing close to the Ruined City and into the Valley of Tholgah-Loh, a sheltered depression set in the foothills of the Mountains of Kappah. Their arrival in Tholgah-Loh marks the end of the yearly migration; a time for rest and repair.

The Mahoudhas are unharnessed and turned loose to graze amid the broad pasture-lands of grass and scrub-thorn, to replenish their strength after their long journey, and to give birth to their calves. Shigger organises his people into work groups, each crew given specific responsibilities: the males fell selected borga-trees, plane the wood into planking lengths, and cure it to effect repairs on the Yurda; the females dig and harvest the long-keeping Juber-root — the main vegetable staple of the Maj-Dron — which they slice into strips to dry on open-framed string lattices for next year's provender. In the evenings, the families gather around their campfires: the females spin and weave the Mahoudha wool for tents, for rugs, and for clothing; the males smith and dress their personal selection of gems from Kazm Ori.

It is also a time for feasting and celebration, for which preparations are made in advance. The males collect the wind-dried berries of the scrub-thorn, which are steeped and brewed in large wooden vats; the females distill the potent fermented liquid from the vats into individual kegs.

While in Tholgah-Loh, the Maj-Dron are visited by Moplos, representative and courier of the Krystellate Obelisk. He delivers my correspondence to Shigger, communications from the Council of Wizards, and fired-clay jars of herbal potions and medicinal sachets sent by the wizardess Wodema. In return the Maj-Dron tender their collected Krystal, any salvaged machinery for Rueggan, and Shigger's yearly report of their migration.

On one such occasion, night was lowering across the Valley of Tholgah-Loh when Moplos led his Gowdan pack-animal, Mos, out of the grey twilight into the encampment. He was a half day early and, had he known what was soon to transpire, he would have gladly delayed his arrival till the morn.

Moplos is a member of The Om-ba-Don, a race three times the height of the Maj-Dron, who prefer the peace and relative isolation of their homeland in the high reaches of The Kappah. Only his dedication to the Great Design of the Krystellate Obelisk allows Moplos to tolerate the noise and chatter of the high-spirited, ebullient Maj-Dron, whose rowdy enthusiasm this evening was further fuelled by copious draughts of freshly-brewed Thorn-Beer. He was surrounded instantly by a throng of excited youngsters who began climbing up his bole-like legs and swinging from his thick waist belt. With stoic gentleness, he tolerated their intrusion upon his massive frame.

Shigger had been notified upon Moplos's entrance, and quickly presented himself to shoo the children away. "Moplos! It is good to see you again! Aren't you early?"

"Better to be early. An Om-ba-Don is never late."

"Early or late, Moplos, having you with us is always a pleasure. Come and rest and talk with me of The Kappah and the progress of the Krystellate Obelisk." Shigger led him towards a Yurda laden with the Thorn-Beer. "Let me offer you some refreshment. I believe you have never tried our drink."

"No time; I need to return."

"But you have plenty of time Moplos. Look! My people are still unloading your Gowdan. Before repacking his panniers, they will curry and groom him; and then he'll be fed and watered. At least let me offer you similar hospitality."

"Well . . . Perhaps one drink to wash the dust and sand from my throat."

"Help yourself, Moplos, please." Shigger motioned with his hand, indicating a ladle beside the beer keg.

Moplos did not even notice the ladle but hoisted the entire keg and, in one quaff, downed its contents.

"Oh, Moplos . . ." Shigger gasped and covered his mouth with his hand. ". . . Oh, Moplos, I don't know . . ."

Moplos appreciatively smacked his lips. "Good!"

Shigger frowned in concern and checked Moplos in a visual inventory for outward signs of effect from the Thorn-Beer. "Perhaps you should sit down, Moplos. Maybe stay the night. Maybe a day. Maybe a few days I think."

"No. No time. No time to waste," Moplos addressed two Shiggers. "I never knew you had a twin brother."

"Maybe a few days I think," deemed Shigger with a pensive nod.

Fog glazed over Moplos's unfocused eyes. "Uh . . . I leave you now," he said, tilting slowly backwards. With a thunderous crash, he fell to the floor. "On second thought, I think I might stay a while longer," he said with a satisfied smile, "Just a while mind you; just a while . . ."

Shortly thereafter, Moplos delivered Shigger's parchments to my door. "Kephren," he asked, "did you not journey some time with the Maj-Dron in your youth?"

"Yes, my friend; I did indeed. Why do you want to know?"

The Om-ba-Don shuffled self-consciously from foot to foot, raising a cloud of dust. "Oh, it's nothing really," he vaguely replied. "I just wondered if you were with them in Tholgah-Loh?"

"That's where I first joined them. Why?"

"Umm . . . well, I thought you might have . . ." Moplos paused and adjusted his backpack.

"Well?" I pursued, wondering where this were leading.

"Did they . . . err . . . give you anything to . . . umm . . ."

"What?" I was becoming a little exasperated.

"To . . . um . . . drink?" he asked, now feigning an air of casual interest.

"Yes, of course. Water, Mahoudha milk and Thorn . . . Ah-ha! Thorn-Beer," I said slowly. "Why? Did they give you something to drink?"

Moplos nodded, looking suddenly guilty.

"Thorn-Beer?"

He nodded again in affirmation and studied his feet.

"One ladle?"

"Err . . . no."

"Two?"

"No."

"Three?"

Moplos said nothing.

"More?"

He nodded.

"How much more?"

"A keg. The whole thing. All of it."

"A keg? A whole keg?" Was this, I wondered, a complaint or a boast?

"I'm afraid so."

"Good Heavens, Moplos! One ladle, yes. Two ladles, maybe. Three ladles if you're really not intending to move for a couple of days. But a whole keg!"

"I know, I know," said Moplos, apologetically. "It's

terrible. I'll never be able to look anyone in the face again."

"Why? What did you do?"

"I am in disgrace."

"Why?"

"I am ashamed."

"Yes! Yes! So I can see!" I replied, my voice betraying my impatience. "But get on with it! What did you do?"

"Fell over." This in a small voice.

"What?"

"Yes, it's terrible."

I could not help but sympathise with him, for I know well from experience, what just a ladle of Thorn-Beer can do, and Moplos had downed an entire keg. Once I had convinced him that I had suffered likewise and therefore understood, he turned Mos loose to browse and lowered himself down, his back against my keldorr tree.

"Don't lean too hard," I cautioned, surveying his bulk and estimating the strength of my tree.

He could recollect no more than drinking the beer, feeling hot, then cold, then dizzy, and falling to the ground. The rest was a vague blur. He had awoken the next morning surprised to find himself covered against the cold night air by a tent.

"Did you have a headache?"

He nodded and winced as if the memory itself was painful. "Like an avalanche on the loose inside." The chill air of the early morning had soon cleared his head but not, alas, his conscience. Locating his backpack, he had checked to see that the panniers were full and, with Mos in tow, padded quietly out of the camp, taking care not to awaken the Maj-Dron soundly sleeping around the ashes of their campfires. He felt he had dishonoured the noble and proud traditions of the Om-ba-Don; that was the cause of his shame. "To make it worse," he said, lowering his voice and ensuring the Gowdan was out of earshot,

"Mos refused to look at me all day and, whenever I caught his eye, he turned away. I kept recalling over and over the words of the Om-ba-Don Creed." Moplos placed his hand on his chest and repeated the words in a slow cadence:

'In one Om-ba-Don,
See the Om-ba-Don's clan.
In the Om-ba-Don's clan,
See the Om-ba-Don's pride.
In the Om-ba-Don's pride,
See all the Om-ba-Don's gain,
For all the many are but one,
Of the Om-ba-Don name.'

"I feel I am unworthy," he bemoaned.

"We've all done things we prefer not mentioned," I reassured him. "Forgive me, but I am old, and this seemed far too innocent a transgression for such depth of self-recrimination."

"An Om-ba-Don does not violate the Creed. Our strength comes from it." He started to repeat the Creed, "In one Om . . ."

"Did your Clan Elder have anything to say?" I quickly interjected.

"No," Moplos replied glumly. "No one knows. I think Mos is too embarrassed to tell anyone."

"He will surely forgive you," I answered, whilst trying to remember if I had ever heard of a Gowdan actually speaking. I could not decide, definitely.

"'Strength of will is greater than strength of hand', according to the great Clan Elder Ptamon III of the Sept Toth of the Clan Tannah." he quoted disconsolately.

I was seriously afraid I might scream aloud. Gritting my teeth, I asked, "But you will never behave like that again, will you?"

"Certainly not!"

"Therefore your will is stronger than ever," I pronounced, quite pleased with my reasoning and mentally complimenting myself.

"It is?" Moplos looked at me hopefully, but a little unsure.

"Undoubtedly!"

"I never thought of it like that. Why, thank you Kephren!"

"Glad to be of help," I said, thankful I would be spared another rendition of the Om-ba-Don Creed.

"I feel much better now," let out Moplos, sounding positively lighthearted as he rose to his feet. He whistled a few notes and his Gowdan came trotting towards him through the trees. "Come on Mos; we've still got appointments to keep!"

I watched with some relief as they trod together into the fading distance. Yet even when they were out of sight, I could hear Moplos start in his deep booming voice:

'In the Om-ba-Don's pride,
See all Om-ba-Don's gain . . .'

I still had not escaped.

In the Mountains of Kappah, the tracts between the wooded lower slopes and the snow covered peaks are known as The Reaches.

Here, the granite flanks of the mountains are open and exposed to the full force of the weather, and little grows save for a few wind-weary stunted trees clinging to silver-grey patches of loose scree. But where the mountains touch shoulders, sheltered clefts and hidden plateaus nestle, shielded by the sheer rock walls from the abrasive lash of the wind. This is the domain of the Om-ba-Don.

Over the course of many years, the Om-ba-Don have improved upon what nature has provided. They have built stone-walled terraces within these mountain folds to trap the mineral rich silt brought down by thawing melt-water, and enable a variety of hardy vegetables and fruit-bearing plants to be successfully cultivated. Some of these terraces are so extensive they appear as flat meadows. The Om-ba-Don plough and work the light soil into a surprisingly fertile tilth, using their pack-animals and, when necessary, even themselves to pull the heavy metal-sheathed ploughshares.

From below the terraces appear as a flight of giant steps ascending the mountainside and, only as each successive tier is broached, do the tended fields become visible. The melt-water seeps through each terrace in turn and the run-off is channelled into rock-lined ditches sunk into the ground. These discharge into natural furrows which deepen and become more pronounced in the course of their descent as the volume of water they carry increases. Finally, far below the bottom terrace, further down the valley, these flumes converge into a wide and deep ravine. The torrent is not wasted; where the slopes decrease in grade the Om-ba-Don have built great dams of stone and scree. The water, thus checked in its downward rush, is backed up and spills over the canyon walls, swelling into a lake of considerable size and depth, its level maintained at the height of the dam.

In such lakes swim a variety of fishes which the Om-ba-Don net and spear. Some are consumed soon after capture, either filleted and cooked, or used as a base for a rich and fortifying broth. The remainder of the catch is preserved to provide stocks for winter when the lake freezes over. Packed in snow, it is stacked in large circular buildings solely from slabs of ice hewn from the permafrost of the mountain heights.

Near the margin of each lake, usually upon some natural hillock cut off by the rising flood, but sometimes on a specially created island, the Om-ba-Don construct their Tarnholds. Imposing rectangular fortifications, they are reached from the lake shores by means of raised causeways breached by a drawbridge which can be quickly raised whenever danger threatens.

When winter descends upon the Kappah, freezing soil of the terraces iron-hard and transforming the meadows into plains of dazzling white, the Om-ba-Don leave their holdings and make their way down to the Tarnholds. Nowadays, thirty two of these buildings house the Clans of Om-ba-Don safe and secure against the severe cold.

Each Om-ba-Don belongs to a closely-knit family, which in turn belongs to a Sept — a group of seven families presided over by a Sept Elder. Each Sept belongs to a larger group of seven comprising a Clan. Thus, seven families make a Sept, seven Septs a Clan and thirty two Clans the entire race of Om-ba-Don. From the ranks of the Sept Elders are chosen the Clan Elders who represent their Clan at Great Assembly. Here, all laws are decreed and decisions directed under the supervision of the Arch Elder, to whom all Om-ba-Don swear their alleigance.

The Septs work their own designated terraces throughout the three seasons, existing on produce grown

Graffyn the Wizard tests an incantation while balancing the Krystal on Grunch's head.

by their own labour. At the end of each Harvest, a portion or tithe of their crop is given over to the Clan Elder by his Sept Elders. The size of this contribution is never measured, for it is a matter of trust and honour, and the individuals of each Sept are free to decide amongst themselves the scale of their donation. This produce is carefully stored in well-aired outbuildings and weather-proof barns inside the walls of the Clan Tarnhold where it is held to provide for the members of the Clan during the barren days of winter and, at the discretion of the Clan Elder, to be shared willingly with other Clan Elders whose Septs may have suffered a poor Harvest. I am aware, from my readings of the ancient parchments, that the thickset walls and solid doors of the Tarnholds once kept out more than hunger and the weather.

Before the Krystellate Obelisk and the Great Design were conceived, the Clans of Om-ba-Don waged unrelenting war on each other. The Tarnholds served then as positions of defence or rallying centres from which to launch an attack upon a neighbouring Clan. They were dark days. The Om-ba-Don warriors, asking no quarter and expecting none in return, engaged in bloody battles, wielding their double-headed Clayda Axes and charging against each other with their many spiked Hahton Shields, intent on domination and the appropriation of new territory. Now their weapons are only sported on ceremonial occasions, their blood no longer stains the snow and they live in peace and harmony. It is well. Their strength and steadfastness is better used to contribute to the Great Design.

The change in the fortune of the Om-ba-Don was brought about by the words and wisdom of one who was destined to become the first of all Arch Elders — Thombon. It was he who first set down the laws by which the Clans might govern themselves and prosper, and who mediated between warring leaders until settlement was reached. The laws are still founded upon the two pieces of parchment scripted by Thombon which are now kept in the archive section of the Obelisk library; The Om-ba-Don Creed and The Om-ba-Don Code. The creed is known to you already from the mouth of Moplos. The Code, which applies more specifically to relationships between the Clans, I have translated into Common-tongue and set down here, much abridged.

THE OM-BA-DON CODE

The hand of one Om-ba-Don shall never be raised against another. Any who break this first and most binding of laws shall be refused succour and the company of their kind, shall be banished to the wastes of permanent snows.

No Clan shall bear arms against another race unless they be deigned Common-Foe by Great Assembly.

No new Clan may be formed and carry its colours, no boundary may be altered, no new territory acquired, other than with agreement of all Clan and Sept Elders.

Shelter and sustenance is the right of all. It may not be refused once formally requested.

Mountain passes and routes are held by no single Clan. It is the right of all to travel them without challenge if they pass without weapons or intent to cause strife.

No territory markers may be placed above the line of permanent snows or below Tarnhold.

Since adhering to The Creed and The Code, the Om-ba-Don have enjoyed peace and the respect of all Krystonians.

Any disputes now occurring are of a trivial nature, soon settled by the mediation of the Arch Elder. His decision is final and no argument persists once his pronouncement has been passed. However, a race descended from such proud warrior-stock will always retain certain elements of ancestral character in its blood. Any Om-ba-Don, whilst holding an unshakeable belief in worthiness of his race, will still assert that the Clan to which he belongs is the noblest of all, and a degree of contention persists. Thombon made provisions for this too; far better he decided, to divert these competitive urges than attempt to subjugate them completely. He initiated, to that end, the Games of Olbaggon.

As winter draws to a close the Clans of Om-ba-Don secure their Tarnholds and journey en masse up to Kappah's storm-wracked peaks and congregate in Olbaggon. A natural amphitheatre of barren ground, roughly elliptical in shape, Olbaggon is enclosed by tiers and fault-scarps of rock, behind which the soaring peaks form a crown of summits. Seated on the bare outcrops and ice-eroded ledges, the massed Clans of Om-ba-Don wait for the spectacle of the Games to unfold in the arena below.

Every Clan is entitled to appoint two representatives or Champions, who compete against the Champions of all other clans in tests of strength and endurance; such include log-throwing, giant snowball hurling, arm-wrestling, rock-lifting, and pack animal races. The performance of the Champions is assessed by elders and an Om-ba-Don achieving the highest overall grading is proclaimed the Champion of Champions. His only rewards are the honour of competing, status for his Clan, and the possession of a thick brown cape fringed with rings of solid gold, which is his to wear thereafter for a year.

The spectators roar encouragement, blow fanfares upon long horns and beat out resonating drum rolls upon hollow logs, urging their Champions to ever-greater feats of strength. Their noise may reach such volume that it can plainly be heard among the foothills far below, or cause the snows on surrounding peaks to shift and slide.

The reports which record the history of The Games in chronological order show that only a handful of Champions have succeeded in winning the cape more than twice before being usurped by a younger, stronger challenger. This puts into perspective the achievement of Bolgon of the Sept Tark of Clan Goll-Tammon, who remained undefeated for a period spanning twenty years. So complete was his domination that on the occasion of his twentieth triumph, the Elders presented him with the cape to keep as his by right and ordered a replacement to be made. Fortunately for his rivals, Bolgon chose that moment to announce his retirement from competition; but not before bowing out with a demonstration of awesome strength and prowess.

The gateway to Olbaggon is marked by two jagged pillars, each twice the height of an Om-ba-Don. It was to one of these that Bolgon strode, clasping it tightly and heaving it from the ground. To the astonishment of those watching he walked determinedly into the centre of the arena and there set the great rock down. "There were Champions before," he had thundered, "and more are yet to come; but let none call himself true Champion until this rock stands again at the gate of Olbaggon!"

Bolgon retired to live out his days working the terraces of the Sept Tark and never again attended The Games. But on their return from Olbaggon, members of his Clan would always find him waiting to ask if the rock now stood at the gate. Always they would shake their heads and reply that the new Champion had tried and failed, and that the rock still remained where he had placed it. Bolgon would give a wry smile and turn his attentions back to his crops.

He would never live to hear a reply to the contrary and he passed away knowing he had no equal during his lifetime. The rock in the arena of Olbaggon was a testament to his life and a reminder of the greatest Champion of all. Bolgon's Rock became the ultimate test of strength.

Fifteen years and fifteen Games passed after Bolgon's demise before a youthful Moplos of the Sept Gomm of Clan Brekk-Darr stepped out into the mountain arena. He had earned the right to represent his Clan, having surpassed the strength of his peers at every stage of selection and his Clan Elder, Bandor was quietly confident that, for all his lack of years, he might spring a surprise. Bandor's confidence was to prove well founded.

Moplos made a clean sweep of events, much to the euphoric delight of his Clan. Having defeated all-comers in the rock-lifting contest, traditionally the last event of the Games, he lumbered over to Bolgon's Rock. The spectators fell silent; only the low moan of the wind above their heads disturbed the atmosphere of tense expectation.

As Moplos took a firm hold and began to slowly straighten, there came the sound of grating rock and, moments later, daylight appeared beneath the displaced gatepost of Olbaggon. Moplos's grunts of exertion were drowned by a standing ovation of deafening cheers, drum rolls, and hornblowing. Every Om-ba-Don hoped to witness at last the rock being restored to its rightful position.

Bent beneath the weight of his burden, Moplos took two paces forward before setting the great rock down. Sighs of disappointment were followed closely by a second round of applause.

He bowed to signify the trial was over, ascended the steps to where the Elders sat and received the cape with reverence upon his outstretched arms. His had been an incredible debut, but there were many who left Olbaggon to prepare their terraces for The Reawakening who saw Moplos's feat, worthy though it was, as something of a failure. After all, they reasoned, had Bolgon not heaved the rock from the gate to the centre of the arena in one unbroken movement?

For the next eighteen years Moplos compounded his first victory, each time culminating in his shifting of the rock two paces closer to the gateway. Upon receiving the cape from the elders, he always declined to wear it as was his unquestionable right. "It does not yet fit my shoulders," he would respond evasively to any query on the matter.

Moplos equalled Bolgon's record of twenty successive triumphs the following year, before covering the half dozen remaining paces to the gateway and finally replacing the pillar to thunderous applause. Again he took the cape and refused to place it round his shoulders even though, by unanimous consent of the Clan Elders, it was his to keep forever. He further echoed the late Bolgon by announcing his retirement, a decision he refused to retract despite protracted pleas from Bandor and the Elder of his Sept. For one who had received the highest of all Om-ba-Don honours, he seemed surprisingly perturbed.

The celebrations at the Tarnhold of Clan Brekk-Darr went on unbroken for the next two days — an unpredicted postponement of returning to work on the terraces which reflected the importance his Clan placed upon their Champions achievement. He took no part in the merriment and, for most of the time, stayed alone in his quarter, where, deep in thought, he sat stroking his hand through the cape's thick hair.

Bandor came at length to seek him out and inquire why he was absent from his own celebration.

"It is not mine alone," replied Moplos. "The honour belongs to all Brekk-Darr."

"But why do you choose to sit by yourself away from

those who speak your name with such pride?"

"I think."

"Of what?"

"Of the cape . . . of Bolgon."

"What of Bolgon?"

"The rock. I do not know if it were my right to replace it. Bolgon can no longer compete, yet I have removed his challenge. He cannot respond. Does that not mar his name and the pride of his Clan?"

"That is the way. All things will change in time."

"I'm not sure they should," said Moplos, still stroking the cape.

Bandor rested a hand on Moplos's shoulder. "Had it not been you today it would have been another next year, or the next. The choice was not yours to make. Come, join your Clan and rejoice with them in our pride."

"Later," Moplos said flatly. "I mean you no disrespect, but I must think yet a little while longer."

"As you wish," conceeded Bandor, withdrawing from the room.

Whilst the Brekk-Darr sang and recounted Moplos's victories until well into the night, a lone figure moved out of deep shadow near to the gateway of Olbaggon, drew a pillar from the ground and slowly, slowly heaved it out into the arena, whereupon he set it down and melted away in the night. Only the mountains saw. Next morning, Moplos was seen wearing the cape of the Champion of Champions about his shoulders for the very first time.

Krystonia shows many contrasting faces, mountain heights and plunging valleys, arid desert and lush forest, searing heat and unbearable cold. Such opposites in the nature of the land are reflected in the diversity of the races which have come to dwell upon it. Nowhere is this clearly apparent than in the Mountains of Kappah, for here live both the towering trunk-limbed Om-ba-Don and a race of creatures so small that one could sit quite comfortably in the palm of Moplos's hand.

The Snow-sprites, now more commonly referred to as Bobolls, inhabit the upper edges of the Om-ba-Don Reaches, where the lands of permanent snow begin. They make their homes in small domed holts, fashioned from hard-packed snow. These single-roomed chambers can only be detected for a short while after construction, for their outline is soon disguised by a fresh fall of snow and becomes lost amid the whiteness of existing snow-banks and drifts. Each holt is accessed by any one of several hidden snow-burrows which meet in a single twisting and confounding tunnel leading, sooner or later, to the Bobolls' dwelling-chamber. In view of their exposed and windswept location, these homes are cosy and draught free, lined from ceiling to floor with a living wall of agum-moss whose only requirement is periodic trimming. The floor is further overlaid with an insulating bed of fresh sweet-smelling grass while perfumed posies of delicate mountain flowers hang down from the curved ceilings, filling the holts with their delightful fragrance — especially fine when certain blooms are in season and have only lately been picked. Radiating from the main tunnel, a network of secondary passages feeds into broad, ice-walled walkways along which the Bobolls may travel unseen, keeping in close contact with their many kith and kin. In this way they pass on news in a continuous, unbroken stream and any event occurring at one end of the Kappah soon becomes common knowledge at the other. The Bobolls have earned their reputation as useful sources of information, which they give willingly if kindly disposed towards the enquirer.

Bobolls are covered all over in short but extremely dense white fur, save for their hands and the very tips of their toes. Such colouration, coupled with their diminutive stature and below-the-snow thoroughfares, means they are rarely seen unless by choice. What's more, the insulating properties of their coats are such that they can avoid unwanted attention by burying themselves inside snow drifts and remaining there for many hours, impervious to the cold. This is rarely necessary for, being generous and good-hearted creatures, they quickly befriend any of a similar disposition; there is much truth in the maxim, 'a friend of one Boboll is a friend to all Bobolls'.

Conversation with Bobolls can be difficult. They have retained their own language — a rapid, guttural flow of sharply accented sounds and soft whirring noises which I still cannot imitate successfully — and, apart from a few individuals who have troubled to learn Common-tongue, they make their wishes and intentions known by means of hand signs, gesticulations, and explanatory diagrams scratched upon the surface of the snow. Communication is further slowed by two characteristics which would soon identify a Boboll to any who might never have encountered one before; their inability to refrain from giggling and their remarkable talent for what Rueggan terms 'Instant Spacial Translocation' but they themselves call 'zumping'.

In all but the most dire of circumstances, a Boboll will soon discover some source of amusement and interrupt any conversation with a protracted fit of giggling. Once he starts, he is not easily stopped and attempts to dissuade him usually heighten and prolong the hysteria. When in this condition, a Boboll is prone to displaying an involuntary sequence of 'zumps'.

Whilst the more practised members of the Council of Wizards can effect a disappearance and then materialise some distance away, it involves much Krystal-induced power, the speaking of complex incantations, and a series of safeguard spells. Even after extensive preparations, such magic is fraught with danger and has seldom been attempted since The Great Gadzoot (who was particularly disposed to disappearing) vanished and never returned. Yet the Bobolls can vanish, or 'zump', at will!

The advantages of such a talent are obvious, and many Bobolls owe their skins to being able to 'zump' out of any tight scrape. It often gets them into one in the first place, however, as they seem to have little control over the location of their reappearance; they are pastmasters at making excuses for a sudden intrusion into another Bobolls holt. Though the distances involved are never large, they must frequently execute a series of 'zumps' to move a short way in the desired direction after 'zumping' down from the tops of trees or out of snow-banks or wherever else they may happen to be. Prolonged 'zumping' requires great expenditure of energy; it is not uncommon for a Boboll to fall asleep on its feet after a lengthy bout of 'zumping'.

My own dealings with the Snow-sprites are restricted to those who dwell in the mountains adjacent to the forest of Keldorran. Of these, Poffles and Trumph are the most familiar to me. A game has evolved in the course of our association, of which they never seem to tire. After leaving a freshly-picked bunch of flowers upon my doorstep, the two Bobolls will bang on the door, scurry away and observe my reactions from hiding. Always, I open the door and feign surprise at finding the gift. Always, I pick up the flowers, press them to my nose as if to test their bouquet and then break into a mock fit of sneezing. Always, the two Bobolls give their hiding place by giggling with mischievous glee. Always, having located them, I go through the motions of administering a stern scolding with a degree of difficulty which depends only upon the pressure of my current workload and not their attempts at concealment!

Poffles is quick of wit and one of those rare Bobolls capable of conversing fluently in Common-tongue. This is offset by an utter lack of control over his frequent and protracted outburts of mirth, and I always allow time for interruptions when attempting to glean from him information. Trumph is larger and exceedingly rotund, no doubt as a result of his passion for food. He can be distinguished far off from other members of his race, not only by his bulbous outline but by the small blue waistcoat he always wears. This he procured in an attempt to conceal a circular patch in the middle of his belly upon which no fur will grow. Poffles attests that this bald-spot is due solely to Trumph's stomach scraping against rough ground when he sneaks about on his hands and knees. I know not if this is true, or why Trumph continues to wear his waistcoat, so conspicuous against the prevailing whiteness of his homeland, now that all the buttons are lost and it no longer conceals his belly.

All Bobolls co-operate with the wizards and make their contribution to the Great Design, not least by finding Krystals in the course of their excavations under the snow. These they turn over to one of the Om-ba-Don couriers or, when convenient, deliver them to the Krystallate Obelisk by hand.

Poffles and Trumph have long been highly regarded as Krystal-procurers of note. From small beginnings when both discovered they had a knack for finding more stones accidentally than others of their kind, they have diverted their energies to actively sequestering them. They frequently make their best hauls by plundering the Krystal hoard of an avaricious individual called Myzer.

Between the weather-smoothed foothills of Kappah and Keldorran's tall trees lies a swathe of open ground where long and sun-yellowed grass whispers the words of a constant gentle breeze. It is here, upon a low rise, that the wood and stone house of Myzer stands.

From between the cracks and through the knotholes of his permanently shuttered windows, he is afforded uninterrupted views in all directions. He can thus be sure that no prying eyes are in the vicinity before undoing each of twenty locks and bolts upon his front door and venturing outside. Although these forays are usually short, both in distance and time spent, Myzer nearly always returns with new Krystals to add to his hoard. His ability to find the stones amid the waist-high grass is uncanny. Some have said he is possessed of extraordinarily sharp eyesight. Yet others claim he can actually smell out the Krystals. I have tested this latter theory on Groc the Trolle, whose sense of smell is legendary; he assures me that the stones smell only of the ground on which they were found and have no intrinsic odour.

Myzer is generally disliked for his greedy ways and for his refusal to lend support to the Great Design. Respectfully approached by delegates of The Council on several occasions, he has steadfastly declined to open his door, responding to all such overtures by bawling through a crack in the shutters, "Go away!" or "Leave me in peace!"

On hearing of Myzer's umpteenth rejection of a representative from The Council, Poffles and Trumph decided that filching from him was a legitimate pursuit; they began to appropriate Krystals for the wizards by raiding his voluminous wood-panelled store-chest. Neither the solid walls of his house nor the heavily chained and padlocked chest are any deterrent to 'zumping' Bobolls and the bemused Myzer now counts a hoard which never grows, regardless of how many new Krystals are added.

Depriving Myzer appears to fulfill some deep-seated need in the Snow-sprites for excitement and adventure, though it must be said that his chances of ever apprehending two little creatures who can vanish at will before his very eyes are slim indeed. The risks involved in the activities of Poffles and Trumph are often of their own making, usually resulting from shortcomings or miscalculations in their 'zumping' techniques. To illustrate my point more clearly, I will cite the incident when Trumph lost the buttons of his waistcoat.

One day, having 'zumped' through the wall of Myzer's house, Trumph materialised under his bed and, to the Boboll's consternation, found himself trapped between floor and mattress, in whose fabric his buttons were inextricably enmeshed. Under normal circumstances he could have promptly 'zumped' his way out, but the buttons fixed him so firmly that wherever he went the bed was sure to follow!

On hearing Myzer's footsteps approaching outside, Trumph kicked and strained in the confines while Poffles tugged forcefully at his arm. And then, just as Myzer turned the handle of the door, he shot free like a stone from a Maj-Dron's sling, with a belly scuffed sore and without a single button remaining on his waistcoat.

Perhaps it was the relative ease with which the Bobolls subtracted Krystals from Myzer that first led them to seek a bigger challenge. Whatever the reason, their decision to attempt a raid upon the stronghold of N'Borg was, to my mind, foolhardy and reckless. It is a wonder they still wear their skins, for if N'Borg's forces had been a little less surprised to see them in their midst, the two diminutive adventurers would surely not have survived to tell the tale.

As it was, they escaped with nothing of value apart from their very lives.

Krak N'Borg stands at the heart of the cold and desolate Waste of Shugg, a region of ice-fields and glaciers, razor-backed peaks and saw-toothed ridges, to the north of Keldorran. For how long it has been in existence is known only, perhaps, by the Evil Lord himself. Yet, I feel certain, the hands which built its soaring turrets and crenellated walls were moved by hearts and minds as black as the basalt blocks they laid. It is a place where nothing of virtue prospers; where all things good wither and die and none mourn their demise; where but the twisted and malformed survive; where only the seeds of evil germinate and bear fruit.

The Krak is no small fortification on the scale of an Omba-Don Tarnhold; even the thirty levels of Krystellate Obelisk would be dwarfed by impregnable ramparts.

Inside, dark courtyards and cloistered quadrangles are hemmed in by sheer walls in which sharp-arched doorways are set, giving access to cold corridors, each one just like the next, where the smallest murmur echoes and moans. Flights of steps appear unexpectedly from the pervasive gloom, rising into pitch-darkness or descending into depths where the darkness lies in brooding expectation. What little light finds entry through the narrow window-slits is a weak and pale cousin of the sunlight which often bathes the peaks of Kappah; and the flames of smoking torches which at intervals dot the walls, burn with little heat. The countless rooms which open off the corridors are mean and uninviting.

The true ethos of Krak N'Borg is best perceived from one of its many turrets, ascended by spiralling staircase, the furthest towers lost from sight, shrouded in a grey pall of ice-haze.

The occupants pass far below like busy insects carefully

picking their way round the heaving maw of a sleeping monster. Shouts of pain, of command, of anger, echoing dull from the excessive walls, come from unseen mouths in unseen rooms and yards. And the Krak itself; as dark, as cold, as unmovable as the mountain from whose rock it was conceived.

As Poffles and Trumph discovered, the sheer enormity of the Krak is enough to make anyone feel intimidated by real or imaginary danger. When they found themselves standing beside a circular opening in the outer curtain wall — one, I surmise, of the Krak's ventilation flues — they had, they freely admit, at least one second thought. Had they been older and wiser, they might have paid heed to the warning voices of their consciences and turned away. But stand those young in years and light of heart next to a hole in a wall and the outcome is inevitable. Poffles and Trumph climbed into the flue.

N'Borg, it seems, rarely converses with any but N'Grall and N'Chakk, whom he charges to carry out special assignments or to pass on orders to the commander of the Krak's forces, General N'Tormet. He in turn delegates to the hundred brutal, broad-shouldered, pike-bearing Honji Officers, who dictate to the rank and file Legions of Snords. The latter do as they are told and provide N'Borg with an incalculable number of dim-witted, axe-swinging, hog-faced footsoldiers, fully prepared to do anything in his name. They are exercised, drilled, flogged without cause, made to sleep overcrowded in stinking sheds, given left-over food in some stage of putrefaction, and set to fight each other to the death for the amusement of their superiors. They follow orders blindly and cry out in adulation whenever N'Borg deigns to honour them with his presence. Such loyalty in the face of their maltreatment is, I think, the truest testament to their lack of intelligence and N'Borg's lack of any feelings akin to decency and compassion.

Myzer gloats over his coveted hoard of Krystals.

I make mention here of the order of things behind the walls of the Krak to signify the dangers to which Poffles and Trumph had foolishly exposed themselves. I shudder to think what such malignant individuals, so accustomed to subjecting their fellows to painful punishment and terrible torture, might have inflicted upon the Bobolls had they taken them into their clutches. By their own admission, Poffles and Trumph came within a whisker of providing them with the opportunity of demonstrating their prediliction to violence, and escaped more by chance than good judgement.

Having spent the best part of a day sneaking between dark corners to avoid detection by Snord patrols in the main corridors, Poffles and Trumph sat down in the cold and damp of a dim retreat beneath a flight of stairs to contemplate what to do next. They had failed to find the expected Krystal-cache and, as Trumph repeatedly complained, anything which remotely looked edible. For all the warmth of their coats, the bitter cold of the Krak had touched them in a way which the most cutting of winter winds on the Kappah could not. Chilled to the marrow and fatigued by extremes of apprehension and relief attending each patrol's coming and going, they were thoroughly disillusioned.

Poffles proposed at length they should retrace their steps and leave the Krak by the same ventilation flue through which they had entered; Trumph agreed, equally anxious to be well away from its walls before nightfall.

They were about to leave their hiding place when approaching heavy footsteps echoed through the corridor above, interspersed with the sound of voices. The Bobolls shrank back into the darkness as the footsteps, now amplified by the stair-well, drew closer and a shadow-army appeared to march the length of the opposite wall.

Down the steps above their heads, grunted and jostled a

unit of Snords so many in number that, to Poffles and Trumph, it seemed an age before the last rank of six was engulfed in the mouth of an archway and the sound of marching feet receded.

Poffles suggested abandoning their previous plan and following a safe distance, in the hope that the Snords might lead them to the elusive Krystals. Again Trumph agreed, in spite of his fear, believing it more likely that the guards were going for dinner.

Keeping within earshot of the Snord's tramping feet, but far enough away to reduce the risk of being spotted in the gloom, Poffles and Trumph trailed their unwitting guides through an endless sequence of age-polished corridors, leapfrogging from one nook to the next. So preoccupied were the Bobolls, they paid no heed to their whereabouts and had no way of knowing how to get back to the flue.

The sound of the Snord's footfalls finally changed in timbre, becoming clearer, more distinct, as if it were no longer contained by the corridor's walls but had found some means of escape. And a new note was now audible; the expectant hum of many voices.

The Bobolls rounded a corner where two corridors met and found themselves blinking and wincing as their eyes adjusted to an unaccustomed brightness washing over them. Fortunately, their blindness was momentary, or they might have stumbled over the feet of a Honji who stood with his back towards them, barring the entrance to a vast torchlit hall.

"That," hissed Poffles, withdrawing to an alcove, "must be where they keep their Krystals!"

"That," warned Trumph, whose nose told him no dining-room lay beyond, "bodes ill! Let's call it a day and get out of here!"

No matter how well-founded are Trumph's line of argument Poffles can always be relied upon to talk him round to a different point of view. Surely he could see how senseless it would be to have risked so much for so long only to turn back at the last moment? Just a quick look, the most fleeting of glimpses, a mere eyeblink, was all Poffles wanted. There was no danger . . . well, not really . . . The sooner they took a quick peek, the sooner they could find something to eat and go home.

They inched their way past the Honji sentry and slipped into the hall, only to be confronted by a forest of Snord legs. Denied sight of anything but the fan-vaulted ceiling across which the diffused light-shapes of many torches played, the Bobolls longed for an elevated vantage point which would serve equally well as a refuge.

Gesticulating fervidly from under the tail-tassle of a Snord, Trumph pointed to a huge green boulder fleetingly visible to one side of the hall. The Bobolls wasted no time in scuttling across the stone floor and ascending the rise, its scaled and fissured surface providing ample foot and finger holds.

Had they the luxury of time, in which to consider their actions, the Bobolls might have wodered what such a rock was doing in the hall, and why its texture was vaguely familiar. Perhaps then they would not have been so startled when, having reached its highest point, they felt the boulder move! It was, of course, no boulder at all but an evil-tempered dragon . . . N'Grall!

For an instant nothing happened. The Bobolls stared into the wicked yellow eyes of the dragon, and the dragon stared at them, trembling in awe on his back. Then, with a roar which extinguished a whole row of torches, N'Grall snapped angrily at the Bobolls. Unbalanced by the sudden movement, they toppled off his back and narrowly avoided his second lunge by diving between the legs of the throng of Snords. N'Grall caught glimpses of the Bobolls' white fur and shot at them bolts of flame with complete disregard for the Snords.

Chaos ensued. Hot and bothered, the Snords charged wildly in all directions and their shrieks of panic caused a fall of loose masonry from the high ceiling. The Honji used their pikes to persuade their charges to calm down. The effect was just the opposite; scorched, then prodded and now trampled by their fellows, the Snords howled in pain as they lashed out blindly with their axes increasing the tally of injuries no end. Within moments, the entire hall had been transformed from a disciplined gathering into a seething mêlée, each Snord fighting for his life against every Honji and other Snord in the Krak. In the midst of all this were the Bobolls, Poffles clinging desparately to Trumph's waistcoat for fear of becoming separated as they ducked and weaved through the flailing limbs, 'zumping' for all they were worth.

Ironically, the Boboll's lack of control over their 'zumping' proved this once to be their salvation. With no idea of which way lay the exit, they inadvertently 'zumped' clear of the raging pitched battle and reappeared in one of the corridors attending the hall. Away they ran, as fast as their short legs could carry them until, exhausted, they dropped off to sleep.

It took the Bobolls the rest of the night and all next day to find another ventilation flue which carried the sweet scent of the outside world up to them and masked the stale odour of dank dungeons. They slid down its smooth interior, away from the Krak's crude forces; by then the Snords were charging frantically back and forth, in search of the unidentified intruders with orders from Henchdragon N'Grall to catch them and boil them alive.

Meanwhile, N'Grall scoured the slopes beyond the Krak; circling slowy, he fused screes, melted snowdrifts and sent glaciers careering down valleys in his drive to find the two creatures who had dared to insult him by climbing on his back. He was no beast of burden like those in Cairn Tor!

Poffles and Trumph emerged into the twilight of descending night, unwilling by now to take any more risks. They watched N'Grall from a snow-bank piled high against the Krak's sheer wall until, defeated for once by darkness, he returned to roost on one of the turrets. Only then did the Bobolls steal into the night and begin the long journey back to the Kappah, slightly older but much wiser than when they had left.

Though my days of carefree wandering and adventure are long gone, they still live brightly in my mind. Memories of outlying homelands and different cultures seem to grow ever clearer with time's passing. I have only to shut my eyes and I am young again, snuggered in the cosy lodge of a genial Om-ba-Don and sampling his steaming broth as a blizzard sweeps over the Kappah; or lying amid the sweet grass of Tholgah-Loh, counting the stars until dreams descend. So vivid are such memories, I find little difficulty in recalling events when committing them to parchment. All, that is, except one . . .

In one of my many cupboards I store trinkets and mementos of my youthful wanderings. Among my collection of drawings, diaries, chunks of rock and other items which would have little significance to anyone else but me, rests a flute, no longer than my thumb. It is simply crafted from a length of hollow reed and looks much like those piped by the bands of travelling musicians who pass through Keldorran from time to time; only it is much smaller. And, whilst anyone could cause some sound to issue from the flute of an itinerant musician, none but a Hydro Glyph can play a note upon my tiny reed.

I have seen it played. I have heard its voice and those of countless others combine in wondrous airs which penetrated deep within my mind and soul; music never to be forgotten but which is never quite remembered. Were it not that I can see the tiny instrument before me, I should be certain that what I perceived one evening, long ere I could grow a beard, belonged only to a dream.

Should you follow the River Cauld downstream from its source in the Mountains of Kappah, skirting the eastern edge of Keldorran and shunning the Valley of Wendlock, you would descend to a fertile flatland, the bread-basket of Krystonia. You would likely venture no further for, beyond these broad flood-plains, the river feeds into the Shadi-

Sampi, a lush and languid swamp of stagnant lakes and shallow reed-clogged pools where serpents, whose painful bites bring lingering death, slink and slide over mats of floating leaves. Somewhere deep within its heart exists a wooded island refuge; but no known trail, no safe track can be followed to reach it. What appears to be solid ground may give way beneath the lighest footfall, its owner swallowed up by quicksand or a stinking bog.

On leaving the swamp, the river does not so much flow as seep out along a wide front, before dividing round numerous tree-covered islets in a bewildering network of shifting creeks and channels. This is the Delta, humid and luxuriant, between the swampland and the sea.

Above the Shadi-Sampi, the river runs clear and cold, still sweet with melted snow and ice from the distant mountains. But after finding its tortuous way through the swamp, charged with rotting vegetation and warmed by the sun and hot springs, it meanders through the Delta dark and tepid. It is this seldom-explored wetland of Shadi-Sampi, Delta and the sea with which this account is concerned.

What the Maj-Dron are to the Cluod-Hakkom, the Gadazorri are to the sinuous waters of the Delta and the coastal regions of the sea. They too are nomadic, their movements following a long-established pattern; but their travels are dictated not only by the changing seasons but by the rhythm of the tides.

The Gadazorri spend near enough their entire lives afloat, only setting foot on land to trade, replenish supplies and effect repairs to their vessels or build others anew. Their craft are constructed to a traditional design which has remained unchanged for generations. The long Rahpans, sleek and elegant ships of single square-rigged sails, are home to extended families including second and third cousins. Their hulls, expertly woven from tightly banded reeds, endow them with lightness, buoyancy and the shallow draught required to navigate shallows and shoals when heavily laden. Each Rahpan, identical in size and shape to every other in the fleet, is distinguished by a singular colour-combination of horizontal bands blazoned proudly upon its sail. The decks are planked with roughened timbers that prevent its crew from slipping in heavy seas, when waves break over the upturned prow. Running the length of each ship, from bow to stern, are the rowing benches, ten to starboard and ten to port. When becalmed, a frequent occurrence in the coastal waters which the Gadazorri ply, the crew sit three to an oar and scull in time to the monotonous beating of a great and resonant drum.

Towed between ports behind every Rahpan are three or four tender boats, or Skeats. The Gadazorri use these little craft for trading, their size and manoeuvrability making them well-suited for landing at the settlements. They are rigged with single lateen sails and, whenever the need arises, they too can be rowed by a compliment of up to six. They have no decks, but are fitted instead with deep waterproof lockers in which valuable goods may be stowed for safe carriage to and from the shore.

Trading activities take the Gadazorri to many coastal settlements beyond reach of conventional transportation, at which they barter fine cloth, parchments and spices in exchange for fresh fruit, dyes and natural fibres. The tidings, moreover, they bring from far and wide provide an invaluable service to these isolated communities; a regular link which keeps them in touch with developments elsewhere, not least in the Krystellate Obelisk.

Now, having told you something of the sea-faring Gadazorri, I will explain the role they played in the acquisition of my tiny flute and how, thanks to them, I beheld a scene which few others have witnessed, or ever shall . . .

I first learned of the Gadazorri late one evening from

Shad, an old wizard much-travelled himself, after helping him to apply the finishing touches to a dry-stone wall around his new herb garden. I was fond of Shad, not least for the wealth of intriguing stories he told and, I sensed, he was fond of me. Though whether he tolerated my constant tirade of questions because of my youthful enthuiasm or my willingness to work in return, I honestly do not know.

On this particular evening, Shad washed and changed into a robe of the finest quality I had ever seen. It was, in constant light, a deep midnight-purple though, by the flickering flames of his fire, it changed hue with his every slightest movement. Thinking how I too should like to possess such a splendid robe, I naturally enquired from whence it had come.

"A gift from Valdar, the Gadazorri captain," he had replied, before proceeding to unfold a fascinating tale of how he came to be travelling aboard the ship of Captain Valdar. He spoke of settlements unknown to me, of skirmishes with hostile sea-creatures, of flat calms and terrifying storms which brewed up from nowhere and threatened to capsize the vessel as it ran in haste for cover. His most lasting impression was clearly of Valdar himself; strong, courageous and implacable, never happier than when threading craft through treacherous reefs and over submerged sand-banks as though his eyes could penetrate the waves. He, perhaps more than any other individual, had earned Shad's lasting respect. It was towards the end of this remarkable voyage that Valdar presented Shad with the fair robe which he now wore, in recompense for his uncomplaining hard work at both helm and oar, and the odd spot of timely magic.

"I only wish," Shad had added wistfully, "I could have stayed much longer. Valdar, you see, believes implicitly that the oceans have no end and that, by sailing west towards the setting sun, he will not drop off into oblivion but return one day from the east! Had he managed to convince enough others to share the courage of his conviction and help build a vessel fit to ride an ocean storm, he would have set sail by now for sure. And I would have gone with him, really I would."

So inspired had I been by Valdar's vision, I decided that I too would seek out the Gadazorri, earn a purple robe of my very own and, should the opportunity present itself, sail beyond the edge of the sea with the illustrious Captain Valdar. Yet many diversions delayed my journey: some that turned me away from my intended direction; others that merely caused me to postpone my plans for a while. Many seasons had come and gone since my informative evening with Shad before I eventually wended my way to a picturesque settlement on the coast. The Gadazorri, I soon learned with keen excitement, were due to arrive there any day.

I quickly found accommodation and made my way down to the beach. There I sat until dusk, my eyes fixed on the headland across the bay. Next day too, I waited in vain . . . and the next. Then, one morning when the sea was ruffled by a persistent light breeze, I caught my first glimpse of a multi-coloured square rig rounding the cape. A magnificent spectacle unfolded before me as more great sails came in view, until they numbered at least a score.

I was not alone in observing the fleet's approach. Many settlement dwellers had already appeared from their homes laden with baskets of fruit, parcels of dye, bobbins and spools of uncoloured threads, all of which they carried down to the beach.

The fleet came to rest some distance offshore as stone anchor-weights were dropped overboard and took the strain. A flotilla of little trading boats quickly sprang into life, buzzing attendantly round their mother-ships like worker bees around their queen. Decks now swarmed with busy crew, furling the square-rigs and lowering cargo by rope to those in the Skeats since drawn alongside. Once full, these worker-craft were sailed ashore and hauled up the beach by the settlement's eager inhabitants.

The Gadazorri, I noticed, were somewhat smaller of stature than I had envisaged from Shad's stirring tales of Captain Valdar. Not much taller than the Maj-Dron, they were thicker-set and less heavily clothed; like Shad's the robes they wore were of undoubted quality and cut.

For a while I stood apart, content to observe the bustling scene as stalls were set up with goods displayed and bartering began forthwith. Oh, the noise — I remember it well! How, I wondered, could affairs of business be conducted against such a cacophony of raised voices?

The intensity of activity presently began to subside. As the finer details of trading were being amicably brought to a close, I approached the nearest group of seafarers, carefully stowing their new acquisitions in the lockers of their Skeat. I asked the oldest among them who, from the way he was giving instructions I assumed to be of high rank, if he might point me in the direction of Captain Valdar.

"Valdar? He's been gone from us for ages," he loudly replied. "Taken his last voyage. Gone back to the sea."

My spirits dropped, assuming at first that he meant the Captain had already set off for the horizon. "Oh, I understand," I said at length, my spirits dropping even further at the realisation of his true meaning.

"If there's more you'll be wanting to know," he suggested, "you'd best talk with his kin. You can't miss their boat; it's further along with a big purple fish ont' sail."

I thanked him and walked away briskly along the beach, eyeing each Skeat's sail in turn for the purple fish motif. Suddenly I saw it up ahead, wafting lightly in the breeze, matching exactly the pigment of Shad's robe. One of the crew had a noble air which, as I drew near, left me in no doubt that he was in charge. I singled him out and, upon introducing myself, I made my purpose known.

"I am Tallac," he said affably. "Valdar was my father. He always spoke highly of Shad whom I well recall, though I was not very old at the time he sailed with us. If indeed you come amongst us as his friend, you are most welcome aboard my family's ship." He motioned to one of the stately Rahpans at anchor in the bay.

So it was that I boarded the same great ship in which Shad had sailed with Valdar, so many seasons before. I followed Tallac across the deck and through a narrow doorway amidships, whereupon we descended a steep flight of stairs. At the bottom we entered a roomy cabin where the Captain's mother, sisters, brothers and more uncles, aunts and cousins than I can possibly recall, were on hand to receive me with warm regard.

The spareness and functionalism of the deck had in no way prepared me for the unrestrained opulence of my new surroundings. Walls hung with rich tapestries and exquisitely embroidered fabrics depicted everyday scenes from Gadazorri life, all mirrored in the wooden-planked floor's high polish. We dined promptly off mats of tightly woven reed, sitting cross-legged on well-padded cushions, exchanging tales of Shad and Captain Valdar.

Early next morning, I watched the fleet weigh anchor with unfurled sails, not from the beach but from the poop of Tallac's ship. I was gladly sailing with them, having eagerly accepted the Captain's invitation to accompany him and his kinsfolk on their travels for as many days as I wished.

And sail with them I did; for so long that I oft began to wonder whether I had ever known a previous existence. And how much I learned from my hospitable hosts. I was soon able to read the weather signs foretelling a squall and pick out a safe anchorage to ride out its duration; read a nautical chart and navigate by the sun, the moons and the stars; trim the sail and pull an oar; steer a straight course at the helm; locate submerged sandbanks and observe the well-established protocol of barter. I began to feel more accustomed to the pitch and roll of the deck than to the stillness of land when ashore.

"Many thought my father mad," confided Tallac, after I had broached the subject on a rare occasion when we were together alone, "to suggest that a ship could ever be built fit to tackle the wide open sea. But not me. You wait, Kephren; the day will surely come when such a boat is built and then . . . ," his eyes caught mine and he smiled warmly. "Then we'll set sail for the horizon, you and I." We laughed heartily and embraced.

Day after day we travelled the coast, plying our lucrative trade. Late one morning, with the sun approaching its zenith, the fleet dropped anchor some distance offshore. Seeing no settlement and sensing no storm, I sought explanation for our quiescence.

"We must wait for high tide," responded one of Tallac's many uncles. "Not enough water else to enter the Delta. This evening we make for the Shadi-Sampi."

"The swamplands?" I asked, my heart missing a beat. "Why should we want to go there?"

"To trade of course, for spices from the orchids which grow there in profusion, but nowhere else. We do the trip every year, when the tide's at its highest and most orchids, we hope, are in bloom. You'd best go below and get plenty of rest; you'll need it. We've a difficult journey ahead!"

As the day wore on, I was awakened from my slumbers by the motion of our ship; we were underway. Grabbing my coat, I raced up on deck and looked around; like the rest of our fleet, we were steering into the funnel-mouth of the Delta, between two protruding sandpits which marked the River Cauld's beginning and end.

The sails, by now having lost the sea-breeze, fell slack and were speedily furled. We made headway by oar to the sound of many drums until, as the banks began to close in, we dropped anchor. My shipmates made fast their Skeats alongside and loaded them with bolts of cloth, before donning their finest robes. I watched them mingle upon the deck, full of admiration.

"Ah, there you are, Kephren," called out Tallac from amongst them. He soon stood before me, holding out a tunic of crimson. "My sister has made this for you."

Enthralled, I cast off my coat and put the garment on; it fitted perfectly and was, I thought, at least the equal of Shad's purple robe. I thanked brother and sister profusely, feeling our friendship cemented for ever.

In the middle of the afternoon, the entire race of Gadazorri — male, female and child — descended the boarding nets hung over each Rahpan's gunwales in high spirits and, when all were set, cast off. The oarsmen, six per craft, rowed deftly with synchronised strokes, directed by companions at the bows, whose voices seemingly floated before us over the light swell. We slipped forward easily at first, on the back of the incoming tide. But as the tide slackened and the current against us grew stronger, the oarsmen were obliged to pull hard.

The river's deep and expansive mouth seemed to bear no relation to the shoals and confusing medley of twisting channels which lay before us. And yet, with no hint of hesitation nor even the slightest doubt, we continued our steady advance. Our chosen channel soon diverged and we opted for one of its branches as a matter of course. We were presently threading a way between low-flung wooded islands, our passage so narrow in places that overhanging branches frequently rattled the masts and our oars stuck fast in muddy banks. A traveller might explore this maze of seemingly identical creeks and backwaters for days on end and be extremely lucky ever to come out alive. Not so the

Gadazorri; they followed a route handed down from their forefathers with an air of quiet confidence.

We came, now and then, to a placid lagoon where strange bewhiskered beasts raised their glistening heads from the murky depths, inspected us briefly and vanished with scarce a ripple. The air was filled with the dull and dirge-like hum of countless insects, some of which were half the size of seabirds, their brightly coloured bodies catching the fading light like jewels as they skimmed the surface in a blur of translucent wings.

By now the current had slackened to an imperceptible flow and the strokes of the oarsmen were shorter, more precise, in response to a steady stream of directions from the lookouts on our bows. Others repeatedly checked the water's depth by means of pierced weights, securely attached to lengths of knotted rope.

The oars were finally rendered useless and shipped aboard. We inched forward by the concerted efforts of two hefty Gadazorri at each stern; employing their oars as poles with which to punt, they needed all their considerable might to extrude them from the channel's sticky bed.

Above our heads was an unbroken canopy of giant ferns and trees, some of which grew taller than any I had seen in Keldorran. The late evening sunlight above this veil filtered weakly through the leaves, casting all in a twilight world of greens and shades of brown, dimming to black in the shadows. Our every movement, it seemed to me for no apparent reason, was being scrutinised by a thousand pairs of unseen eyes, a sense intensified when I realised that the sun, for so long hidden, had finally set for the night. The shadows seemed at once to visibly swell, driving dull light before them and plunging us into an ever-deepening darkness. How, I failed to comprehend, could we continue our journey safely in such gloom? My unspoken question would very soon be answered.

Pinpricks of green light suddenly winked and gleamed before us. I stood up for a better view and, seeing them stretch far ahead, supposed them to be lanterns affixed upon the trees; two parallel lines of luminescence tracing a corridor through the void along which we could travel.

"The Hydro Glyphs," said someone whose face I could not see. "We're almost there!"

In this dank and dangerous place, there emanated from each lantern an aura of peace and wellbeing so profound, I instinctively knew no harm would befall us while they shone. All sense of time and motion faded away as our boats were enveloped by thick mist, obscuring all but the lanterns along this eerie avenue.

I shuddered slightly as our bows ran aground. "Come," said Tallac at my side. "Pick up a bolt of cloth and follow me."

I did as he requested and, grasping his robe with my free hand, pursued him blindly to dry land. Behind me came the muted sounds of other boats reaching the unseen shore and low voices of more Gadazorri as they approached us through the mist. I soon found myself surrounded by a host of vague figures, robes aglow with that same weird light which had shone so soothingly from the trees. I looked down at the arm of my tunic; it too had turned a shade of green.

"Tallac!" I called out uncertainly.

"Be calm, my friend," his voice answered. "Trust me and do not speak; only follow closely."

How Tallac and his company could have been so sure of their steps, I do not know; perhaps the same instinct which guides them unerringly through the thickest of sea-mists works equally well on land. I could barely see my feet and would surely have strayed into a watery grave had I not fixed my eyes upon Tallac's green-glowing back. We moved onward in total silence, winding our way between trees which loomed out of the mist like the legs of a race of giants.

After an age, we stopped and deposited our rolls of cloth atop a white stone slab. Upon the many Captains' orders, we stepped well back.

For an awful moment I feared I'd been deserted, for all the Gadazorri had faded into the mist. Then Tallac appeared beside me and said softly, "Come Kephren; now we can rest."

I followed him to the base of a nearby tree where we sat apart, wedged between its gnarled and twisted roots. Tallac's head soon bowed forward in sleep; but I stayed wide awake, wondering why we had set down our loads in such an unlikely spot, deep in the midst of the Shadi-Sampi — and in the dead of night! Then the music had begun.

A single note pierced the heavy silence, clear as a bell. Before it died away, another rang out and another, till the mist was filled with sound, each note enmeshed in perfect accord. Still the music swelled, louder and louder as pipes, harps and chimes interweaved enchanting melodies. Then voices. Oh, that I could do justice to the beauty of those voices! Yet I cannot. How am I to explain on parchment that which transcends the endowment of words? This was music the like of which I had never heard and, surely, never will again. It reached out to me and soon possessed my entire frame. The music was the mist, the mist the music and I was part of both — floating on that harmony of sound like our boats upon the water.

The musicians loomed imperceptibly through the mist which shimmered with their graceful movements as I sat back entranced; spiralling upwards and down, ascending, swooping, darting this way and that, leaving broad trails aglow in their wake like soft green ribbons. And as they drew near, those ribbons of light became entwined, spinning a web of intricate luminescence. Suddenly it dawned on me — they had been the lanterns; indeed they were one and the same!

The Maj-Dron migration passes the ruined city at the entrance into the Valley of Tholgah-Loh.

Now, at last, I could make out their forms. Some had the full cheeks of infants. Some, clearly females swathed in long tresses of free-flowing hair, sang and danced with handsome males. And how youthful they all were. I returned their happy smiles with unashamed joy, those Hydro Glyphs of the Shadi-Sampi.

One Glyph, a flautist, touched down upon the lowermost branch of a nearby tree and said to me in high-pitched voice, "My name's Boll. What's yours?"

"Kephren," I replied, still with sweet music ringing in my ears.

"You look tired," said Boll. "what you need is some nectar."

He promptly flew away and only then did I trace the green light's source to his luminescent wings. For how long he was gone I cannot say, but it seemed to me the merest fleeting moment. With him came perhaps a dozen more, each bearing a cup of reddish clay, no bigger than my ink-well. Boll alighted back on the bough, as his fellow-Glyphs formed an orderly queue at my feet. He then clapped his hands just twice.

The first in line stepped forward to my side, her radiant features way beyond compare — full lips, sweet nose and the most appealing eyes which spoke to me of carefree happy love.

"Meet Vena, my queen," said Boll. "Take her cup and drink the goodness therein."

I held out my hand and the fair consort coyly placed the little cup in the hollow of my palm. Raising it unhurriedly to my lips between forefinger and thumb, I let the contents drip out onto my tongue. The effect of those few drops was immediate, though I struggle for words to describe how it felt; my weariness of mind and body flowed through my veins to the ground and left me with a sudden urge to laugh and to leap up and sing. In the nick of time I controlled

myself and showed due respect to my hosts. I thanked the
fabulous Vena, who smiled at me enchantingly before
turning and drifting away.

"This is Ploot," announced Boll as the next Glyph settled
beside me. "He is an elder among us and a dab hand at
playing the harp."

Ploot, to my mind, looked no age at all; a mere slip of a lad
in the fulness of youth. I took up his cup and drank from it.
"Wonderful!" I extolled.

"Now Dillo," said Boll; "Ploot's brother. "Dillo excells on
the pipes . . ."

I drained my cup and began to feel light-headed, a feeling
which grew as each succeeding Glyph approached me and
withdrew.

"And Fioll," said Boll. "She's only a baby as you can see,
and has only just learned to fly. Yet she can already play the
flute quite well, can't you my petal?"

Fioll nodded and gurgled as I took up her cup. When,
moments later, I thanked her, she gurgled again and
beamed a radiant smile, her chubby cheeks dented with
dimples. Then, to my amazement, she hopped lightly upon
my breast and took from her waist-band a tiny flute. She
began to play, all the while regarding me with a look akin to
mischief as her performance held me spellbound. When she
had finished, she gurgled again and, leaning forward, poked
her flute into the pocket of my tunic before floating away
through the mist in fits of joyous laughter.

"Oh, what it's like to be young," grinned Boll with a
twinkle in his eye. "Now here we have Mondo. He oversees
the harvesting of the orchids and keeps tabs on their
yield . . ."

And so it went on, all the way down the line. Each time I
drank the nectar, I felt even younger, lighter, happier,
heartier; and the joy of sweet music entered my soul.

"Here's Lud . . ."

"Now Wanda and Fillan. For some reason which escapes me, they happen to be inseparable and go everywhere hand in hand . . ."

"This is Ria . . ."

"And Taron . . ."

"And last but not least, we have Tan . . ."

By then I felt wholly at one with the Hydro Glyphs and, taking out my flute, I pretended to play. The Glyphs responded zealously and thrilled me with a stunning repertoire of their unbelievable talents. Never before had I known such lightness of spirit; never before had I known such happiness outside the realm of my dreams.

I cannot remember falling asleep, only waking to find that daylight had returned and that the Hydro Glyphs had vanished, along with the mist and the bolts of cloth upon the slab of stone. Yet in their place were many baskets of reed, each stacked neatly to the brim with the seed-heads of countless orchids, their aroma wafting gently through the glade. I did not see a single Hydro Glyph that morning nor even hear its voice; and never have I to this day.

I took my leave of the Gadazorri when we came to our next port of call. It was an emotional occasion; after many embraces and promises to return, I tore myself away with tearful eyes and turned inland for home, proudly wearing my crimson tunic in the pocket of which was the tiny flute.

I must add as a footnote to this account a recent event which may yet confirm the wisdom of Valdar's dream. It concerns an alien tree, espied by a Gadazorri Captain named Tulan, floating on the ebbing tide of a sheltered bay. I am informed that upright, it would have stood taller than his Rahpan's mast, and that its long and deeply indented leaves sprouted not from twigs and branches but radiated out from the very crown.

Tulan and his willing crew hoisted the strange tree on board and counted nine large nut-shaped fruits attached to the trunk beneath the crown. They cut one free and inspected its hairy husk; their attempts to prize it open all failed, till Tulan succeeded in slicing it through with a swift sharp swipe of his hatchet. A liquid spilled out upon the deck, white as a Mahoudha's milk. One of Tulan's several brothers stooped and ran a finger through the milk, sucked it clean and proclaimed how refreshing it was to the taste. The Captain plucked a second nut from the recumbent tree; only this time he drilled a neat hole in its side and poured the milk into a bowl before taking a sip himself. Satisfied, he handed it round. Further nuts were removed, to be drained and cast overboard until, by the time each of Tulan's family had sampled the rare delights within, only one still remained on the tree. This, the largest nut of all, they sent off to the Council of Wizards, care of Dragon Transport Limited.

Several nights did Gos and Ghedra rise and fall before The Council completed the customary sequence of exhaustive tests, pronouncing milk and kernel safe to consume and expressly beneficial to all races. Yet from whence it came to reach Krystonia's shores, few of the wizards would even hazard a guess. Word had long since filtered to the Obelisk of Captain Valdar's dream, but only Rueggan had given it any serious thought; it fell in line with his own hypothesis as to where the sun disappears at night and the moons in the light of day. That single strange exotic tree, he firmly believes, may lead in time to a far-reaching reapraisal of Krystonia's place in the universe. "It is perfectly feasible," he postulated, to the disconcertion of many, at The Council's next full meeting, "that other lands lie far beyond our shores, on one of which grew Tulan's tree!"

Rueggan proposed that he approach the Gadazorri on behalf of all Krystonians, and put before them the exciting challenge of exploring the high seas. "And who better," he suggested, "than Tulan, son of Tallac and grandson of the

legendary Captain Valdar, to lead such an historic voyage?"
To Rueggan's surprise, The Council gave their consent, albeit somewhat reluctantly.

He has lately returned from a short stay in one of the settlements on the coast. Whilst there, he described to the Gadazorri Captains his reasons for propounding such a dangerous mission and was taken aback by their wholehearted support, most of all from Tulan.

Rueggan came back with many ideas to incorporate into his design for a new kind of ship, capable of riding out the mightiest tempest imaginable. He had known very little of my life among the Gadazorri till Tulan's father filled him in and asked, as a favour, to be remembered to me.

"He sends you this message," the wizard called at my home one evening to say, "that a cabin awaits you next to his, as soon as the great ship is ready!"

Until five generations ago, those who worked the magic did so independently, squandering the power of Krystals to satisfy their whims and desires as though the precious stones were as easily found as leaves upon the trees. The consequences were chaotic. One Spell-caster would summon rain in the same instant his near neighbour was calling up warm sunshine. Released in such close proximity, the two spells would often fuse and produce a short-lived but violent thunderstorm — and an equally charged exchange between the two Spell-casters! The more powerful wizards and wizardesses cast fewer spells but of much greater potency; many followed the magical recipes set down on parchments handed on to them by their predecessors, who had used vast charges of Krystal in their magic to achieve spectacular results. An entanglement of this magic, whilst not as frequent, had wider-reaching consequences which were difficult and dangerous to rectify. Eventually, so many spells were being inadvertently meshed and unwittingly blended, it became well-nigh impossible to set an incantation in motion at any time of day or night without it suffering some alteration or corruption. The weather became dangerously unpredictable. It was not uncommon to witness sunshine at breakfast, hailstones by lunchtime and a snowfall just before supper.

There was, among the many accusations and counter-accusations flying around, much talk of finding a solution — and even the occasional half-hearted attempt at agreeing to a timetable. There was, however, no positive plan for remedial action put forward; nor did there ever seem likely to be. In the event, it took a momentous discovery to effect a change for the better.

A young wizard by the name of Azael had, for some time, campaigned for the introduction of a single 'guild' which would incorporate all Spell-casters in a cohesive organised body. He had met with scant success; the magicians were very forthcoming in their condemnation of others but extremely reticent when it came to the idea of sharing details of their private spells. Persistent though he was, Azael had eventually abandoned all hope of ever resolving the situation.

Disillusioned and downhearted, he retreated to a quiet tree-ringed glade, set upon a hill near to the head of the Valley of Wendlock. By walking around the outer edges of the trees, he was afforded views in all directions; to the east, the snow-rimmed Mountains of Kappah roared into the clouds; west, the Valley of Wendlock plunged deep and wide; the trees of Keldorran touched against the hill's north slope and, to the south, he could follow the sinuous silvered ribbon of the River Cauld until it thinned into the nothingness of the horizon, somewhere beyond which lay the Shadi-Sampi. This pleased him.

Inside the knot of trees, Azael fashioned a rough but serviceable shelter from branches and turf beside a sprawling thicket of hedge-bramble which took up much of the glade. There he began to develop his own magic according to a strict self-imposed regimen, determined that he, at least, would be organised.

His spells were frugal in their usage of Krystals, but always approached with care and attention to the tiniest detail. Each, no matter how inconsequential, he logged in a small spell-diary, making exhaustive notes and observations which he felt sure would lead to the advancement of technical knowledge.

Azael's diary grew as steadily as his reputation amongst the inhabitants of a nearby community. They came increasingly to rely upon his limited but effective spells to achieve positive results, rather than on the grandiose magic of the powerful Spell-casters who frequently caused more trouble than they were worth. His shelter soon housed a collection of six spell-diaries and provided a place of rest for the growing stream of visitors who came seeking his assistance.

One such visitor was a wizened old woman who humbly assumed responsibility for the wizard's health and nourishment. She asked no magical favours, but an endless barrage of questions concerning Azael's desire to see all magic unified, all spells collated, and the power of the Krystals used sensibly. His answers to her questions on one particular morning would have historic repercussions.

"I have noted," said she, watching critically, as he hungrily consumed the loaf she had brought for him, "that you always perform your magickery inside this ring of trees."

"Mmmm . . ." Azael mumbled, his mouth full of food and his head full of new ideas.

"Why is that?"

Azael gave a 'who-knows-who cares' shrug, his interest centred upon his breakfast. "Works better," he replied without interrupting his chewing.

"But why? Surely magic is magic regardless of where the spell is spoken?"

"Mmmm . . . you'd have thought so." Azael was grateful for the old woman's food but not her inquisition over breakfast.

"So why do you choose here? Why does your magic fire well when the air is full of more powerful words than yours?"

"Attention to detail," Azael replied, nodding towards the six thick spell-diaries as he brushed the crumbs from his tunic.

"I know what works. The longer a mud-brick lies in the sun, the stronger the house it will build, if you see my point."

"No, I don't."

"Well, its really a matter of . . ."

"Be quiet and eat this," the old woman offered her

adopted wizard a chunk of creamy cheese. "You're thinner than a whip and make less sense."

Azael smiled and accepted the cheese, much preferring her interest in his diet to her questions regarding a wizard's professional business. Breakfast was finished, without further interruption.

Only when Azael's work drew to a close for the day and he sat down to supper did his conversation with the old woman turn over in his mind. At first he thought little of it and after eating, began to write up the day's account of his spells. But her questions tapped upon the window of his consciousness like impatient birds accustomed to being fed at a certain time.

At length, Azael set down his quill and looked out at the dense mass of brambles. The old woman had a valid argument; his spells really did seem impervious to interference, even though he often worked them in the face of magic far stronger than he could produce. Why should this be so? He was sensible enough to realise that it could not simply be explained by his scrupulousness, nor his unwitting possession of extraordinary talent.

Fortunately, Azael was gifted in another sense — he had an enquiring mind. Consulting the earliest entries in his spell-diaries, he recalled working his first spells outside the ring of trees. These had all suffered some impediment, and often his magic had been knocked aside, swallowed up and rendered ineffective by the much stronger conflicting spells of the more powerful wizards. Only when he had begun to conduct his magic inside the brambled glade had he achieved real success. Yet he knew he had never made a conscious decision to do so. It seemed as if he had made the choice unknowingly to forsake all other locations. But why? When? Then, almost as if he had suddenly been awakened from a long deep sleep, he saw clearly.

The old woman! Had she not said from the first time they

met that inside the trees was 'good' ground for a wizard? How often had she looked at him and commented upon the correctness of his ambitions but the blindness of his eyes? "One day, Azael; one day you will see," she had said more times than he could count. And how easy, how familiar his name had sounded upon her lips. The constant enquiries, suggestions, assertions which Azael had dismissed as the idle talk of a lonely old woman began to well up in his mind, threatening to drown him. He had vainly prided himself upon his own careful spell-words and had not even realised the greater message contained in those of the old woman. He was, he told himself, a mud-brick which had lain in the sun for far too long! Whatever imbued his magic with such uncommon power must lie within the glade, somewhere beneath the brambles . . .

He began to strip away the interwined creepers, heedless of the deep scratches inflicted by their cruel thorns upon his arms and hands. The power was here, and he was going to find its source even if it meant uprooting the entire thicket and each surrounding tree!

Azael worked his way deeper and deeper into the dense tangle. Long into the night he yanked and hacked at the creepers, never stopping to question the wisdom of his search. As he approached the very heart of the hedge-bramble, he first noticed a wash of pale light which formed an aura around him. Spurred on, he ripped the creepers away as though they were the flimsy webs of spiders across a long-unentered threshold. Moments later, he stood transfixed as the last thick tendril fell away to reveal a Krystal of staggering dimensions, glowing with a soft light that seemed to pass through him as though he were not of solid form. Azael stared in wonder at a source of power which knew no equal, which all Spell-casters would come to know as the Dom Krystal. The spells he had set since arriving in the glade had, unbeknown to him, been strongly influenced by the mere proximity of this mighty stone. If he were to work spells directly through its heart, the combined powers of every Spell-caster in the land would be unable to check or challenge his intent!

Had he been a malevolent character, Azael could have easily abused his unexpected position of power and kept the discovery secret, using it to quash all others. The thought did not cross his mind; to him, the Krystal was the means by which he could achieve his dream — the unification of all Spell-casters. He was merely an instrument, part of some greater design.

The new dawn was just beginning to etch the trees onto a backcloth of brightening sky when he emerged from the bramble to await the old woman. Did she really know of the Krystal's existence, could she, perhaps, be a wizardess? With these and many more questions to put before her, he realised for the first time that he had accepted her food, dismissed her enquiries and not once taken the trouble to find out her name. Now he felt unable to proceed without her approval and forgiveness.

The old woman did not make her expected appearance with his breakfast. Lunchtime came and passed with still no sign. At supper, Azael was close to panic. After a sleepless night, he set off for the nearby settlement from which he felt certain she must hail.

His arrival and subsequent enquiries served only to heighten his dispair. No woman answering her description had ever lived there, had even been seen in the locality. If her dwelling place was anywhere between there and the Valley of Wendlock, no way could she have escaped their attention. She must live some distance away. Azael questioned those whose faces he recognised as regular visitors to the glade; to his horror, they denied ever having seen her inside his shelter. Yes, they had found him eating a breakfast of bread and cheese on more than one occasion; but a woman standing over him whilst he ate? Never!

Azael returned to the glade, confused and bewildered. He sat, wracking his mind, attempting to solve the mystery, so deep were his thoughts, so intense his concentration, he was overtaken by fatigue and slipped into an exhausted slumber.

Then a dream came; a kaleidoscope of strange visions in which the huge Krystal sat atop a soaring tower; where the faces of those he knew to be magicians smiled and pointed; where the hands of someone whose countenance he could not see moved across a parchment on which strange designs were sketched and numbers were written — they moved as if trying to explain something to him. He could not comprehend; the visions came and faded too quickly, and the dream was empty of all sound. Only the face of the old woman, looming large and smiling between the different scenes, brought him comfort and a link with his conscious life.

When Azael awoke, feeling peculiarly rested and at ease, the sun was already past its zenith. The scratches inflicted by the hedge-bramble were sore and smarting but, much to his amazement, had been thoroughly cleaned and tended. To one side, lying in a small basket, were a freshly-baked loaf and a large wedge of creamy cheese.

Azael's heart sang; the old woman had returned! He dashed outside, expecting to see her waiting for him by the bramble, but the glade was deserted; the dew beneath the shade of the trees, which had not yet been evaporated by the sun's increasing warmth, was undisturbed. Only when he re-entered his shelter, more perturbed than ever, did Azael study the loaf. Embossed in bread-letters upon its golden crust were the words: 'MY NAME WAS ORIA.'

Azael's indecision over the next few days was, perhaps, understandable considering the amount of disruption his usually inflexible routine had suffered. He would sit pondering for hours at a time, make notes and calculations, stand as if satisfied and about to take some action, then sit down again to reconsider, certain there must be a vital element overlooked. More than once he toyed with the idea of forgetting The Krystal's existence and carrying on with life as normal — at least then he might avoid liability if anything went awry. But Azael was a fish well used to swimming against the current, and these doubts soon gave way to more positive thoughts. Yet, as it transpired, Azael would never be required to make the first move. Circumstances unforeseen, which could not have been better orchestrated had they been planned, would carry him along like a fallen leaf borne upon a stream.

After an unusually prolonged period of high humidity and frequent heavy rain, two of the most influential wizards in the Valley of Wendlock had initiated identical spells at precisely the same moment. Both summoned cold winds which, they believed, would clear away the banks of threatening clouds and bring welcome relief from the oppressive heat. Their two spells meshed, becoming one with too intense a power.

The chill wind they had each invoked manifested itself as a high-velocity freezing gale which, meeting the rain-laden clouds, caused a self-perpetuating hailstorm to whip along the Valley of Wendlock and come to a turbulent standstill above the settlement, close to Azael's glade.

The storm wreaked havoc. Krystal-sized spheres of ice showered the settlement, knocking those inhabitants caught outside when it struck to the ground and terrifying those who sought sanctuary in their homes by smashing holes through their ceilings. If the storm was not quickly dispelled, the settlement was destined for ruin!

The two wizards, upon being angrily informed of their error, strove to drive the storm away by combining their power. They failed; it raged on unabated.

In desperation, a small delegation came from the settlement to seek out Azael, having survived the hailstorm barrage by holding a door over their heads as a shield. The sight of the door's battered timbers and the breathlessness of those who had sheltered beneath, left him in no doubt as to the urgency of their errand.

Consulting his spell-diaries, Azael found details of one he had previously used to disperse the light showers which had a habit of appearing whenever he tried to light a cooking fire outside his shelter. Advising the bedraggled onlookers to retreat to a safe distance, he pushed his way into the brambles towards the giant Krystal, to test its power directly for the first time.

A gentle flush of light attended the words of his spell, in contrast to the blinding burst which usually radiated from smaller Krystals on receiving an incantation. He felt sure his words had been too weak, but they were the best he knew how to apply within the framework of limited experience of weather-working. Emerging from the brambles, he informed the delegates of his fears, and suggested they went home in the hope that some improvement may have been caused. They left without delay.

Before they reached their settlement, the storm-clouds suddenly vanished. Incredible; one moment they were being pelted with giant hailstones and the next the sky was blue! They arrived to find their kinsfolk peering out cautiously from doorways and windows, staring up at the sky in wide-eyed wonder. Azael had proved himself, everyone agreed, to be the only wizard worth knowing. Privileged to have him working in the vicinity, they would do all they could to make certain he stayed!

The news of Azael's triumph was not long in reaching the two wizards who were keeping a low profile, closeted in a deep cave. They received it with mixed feelings. On the one hand they were aggrieved at losing face to a local Spell-caster and, on the other hand, relieved that the hailstorm had been vanquished before the thoughts of the settlement-dwellers turned to compensation or, even worse, revenge. This unknown wizard, they decided, must be paid a call. Perhaps then they might discover the source of his great power! whatever was the secret of his success, they wanted it for themselves!

Thus, clothed in their finest raiments, the wizards came to stand outside Azael's shelter, their hats respectfully doffed. Supposing them to be yet another representation from the grateful settlement, he emerged and almost choked on the breakfast he was chewing. Before he could speak, one of the wizards, stately and imposing with heavy black eyebrows and the most luxuriant growth of beard Azael had ever seen, stepped forward.

"I am Gilbran of Wendlock," he said loftily, "and this is Shoof of the same. Please direct us to the renowned wizard who practices The Noble Art hereabouts."

Swallowing the last of his repast, Azael told them there was no wizard to be found in the area who might be called renowned, present company excepted. He feared the two wizards had been sadly misinformed.

"We have been assured," insisted Gilbran, his beard bristling at its edges, "that the one we seek practices here and nowhere else. Make haste and lead us to him. We are busy with other pressing matters and can not stand exchanging pleasantries with such a vagabond as you!"

Azael's face flushed. He was irked by Gilbran's supercillious manner to the point where he considered raising his fists. "As you seem so certain of your information, I can only assume it is I whom you seek," Azael responded cooly, fixing Gilbran with an unwavering stare.

The haughty pair gasped and swopped quick words before Gilbran addressed him again. "You claim to be he who dispelled the storm?"

Moplos the Om-ba-Don leads Mos down the scarp of the Mountains of Kappah.

"Oh, that? . . . Yes it was I," Azael said, as if it had been some trifling matter, hardly worthy of mention.

"Zounds! Gadzooks! The affrontery!" exclaimed Shoof. "The ease with which he lies!"

Before the exchange could deteriorate further, a group from the settlement appeared in their midst. Recognising the perpetrators of the disastrous storm, the newcomers walked past them as though they were tree stumps and placed two large panniers at Azael's feet.

"Please accept this gift, Azael Stormslayer," said a spokesman, "along with our respect and gratitude."

Azael accepted graciously, but thought the 'stormslayer' title was overdoing things a little.

"You deserve this and more," returned the spokesman, quite aware he had the attention of Gilbran and Shoof, "which I fear I cannot say for others who wear the robes of Spell-casters but do not honour them!"

"Hear, hear!" chorused his colleagues and shot the two wizard's withering looks.

"Take my advice," said the spokesman, urged on by his fellows. "Tell 'em to get lost and leave those alone what knows how to do a job proper!" The delegation gave the wizards yet more angry glares before marching out of the glade.

"I think," said Azael quietly to the visibly deflated pair, "we should talk awhile. Don't you?"

"Gladly, Azael Stormslayer" they agreed.

Like it or not, Azael was seemingly stuck with his new name. But in gaining it, he had also found the first two members of what would become, sooner than he could know, the one and only convocation of Spell-casters in Krystonia; The Guild of The Stone Circle.

Gilbran and Shoof were wizards of high status. After leaving Azael, having sworn an oath of secrecy upon their parchments and spellbooks, they travelled the length of the

Valley of Wendlock, telling an account of the young wizard which enhanced his reputation, aroused curiosity, but did not give away too much information. Within days, they collected a considerable gathering of independent magicians and led them into the brambled-glade to hear Azael speak.

Throughout the ensuing discussion, Azael remained judiciously vague whenever reference was made to the source of his power, steering around to topics such as clearing the air of unnecessary magic, conserving Krystal-power and, particularly, the benefits which all might enjoy if only they could agree to work together. Whenever this last subject was broached the temperature of the debate rose sharply, many impassioned speeches being made about loss of freedom and independence. But, as Azael was quick to point out, what freedom was there in working magic which stood little chance of success — surely, greater satisfaction could be found in productive magic.

Azael spoke with the quiet authority and confidence of one far beyond his years, and the Spell-casters were soon paying closer attention to his words than to his dowdy clothes or lack of beard. Finally, having let all voices have their say, Azael took a deep breath and began to clarify his position.

He required all present at the meeting to swear a binding oath upon their spellbooks, guaranteeing their co-operation and willingness to follow his leadership for a period of a single year. If, after that time, they were dissatisfied, they would have every right to replace him with another of their choosing, he would swear a binding oath to this upon his six spell-diaries. If they should seal the agreement, he would waste no time in revealing to them the source of his great power.

Urging the hushed assembly to think hard in coming to a decision, Azael rose and entered his shelter, his countenance composed but his stomach turning and rolling like a butter churn. Everything hinged on the outcome.

Thanks largely to Gilbran's and Shoof's influential support of Azael's proposition, and to the overwhelming fascination the magicians all shared concerning his power, they reached their verdict quickly. By show of hands, they unanimously agreed to his terms; the first real step towards unification of Krystonia's Spell-casters had been taken.

Azael promptly implemented two major decisions.

Firstly, use of The Dom was to be carefully regulated; all Krystals known at that time lost their magical powers eventually, and Azael was impassioned to ensure that The Dom's properties were not exhausted before his vision could be realised. Secondly, he directed tall standing-stones to be placed at intervals of seven paces around the base of the hill upon which stood his tree-ringed glade; these would denote the limits of a sanctuary inside which only members of the new Guild would be permitted.

The huge circle of seven-times-seventy stones was, upon completion, proclaimed by Azael to be the Henge of Oria in remembrance of the old woman to whom, he believed, he owed everything. Beyond, the wizards built their living quarters; the Henge of Oria could not be approached from any direction without at least one Spell-caster barring the way.

After preliminary meetings and an interim during which the wizards tested The Dom with rather weak spells in order to ascertain its potential, the most skilled weather-workers amongst them were selected to formulate a combined spell which, Azael insisted, they carefully log in a newly bound spellbook, so it was that the wizards Gilbran, Shoof and Tagellmohn designed and executed the first major spell through The Dom, making magic to stabilise the local climate.

Within a short space of time, the population in and

around the Valley of Wendlock increased at an alarming rate as the inhabitants of neighbouring settlements; hearing of the favourable conditions to be found there, inwardly migrated. Along with them came a variety of magicians to seek out the unknown core of this great magic. Soon, a swelling settlement of assorted wizards, wizardesses, illusionists, weather-workers and potion-makers were encamped around the borders of The Henge. Azael saw and spoke to them all, setting out the conditions of entry to the newly-termed Guild of The Stone Circle. Most accepted immediately though some, valuing too highly their independence, refused and returned to their old haunts. Azael lost no sleep over them. In time, he knew, they would surely return of their own accord.

But the new magic, beneficial though it undoubtedly was, caused difficulties. If the influx of immigrant settlers continued unchecked, the Value of Wendlock would soon become grossly overcrowded and the rest of Krystonia deserted. Azael decided upon a radical solution which would, if successful, extend climatic control to encompass a much wider area. The Great Spell which was subsequently unleashed spread the extent of The Guild's influence from the snowline of the Kappah to the foothills of Shugg, embracing all lands between these two mountain ranges and the sea. All the peoples of those lands would henceforth enjoy a life ordered around the predictable change in the character of three seasons: Reawakening, Growth and Harvest. Winter, Azael decided, should be a time for resting, when the awesome power of The Dom could be conserved.

The Great Spell stemmed the flood of settlers and accelerated the procession of magicians, exactly in keeping with Azael's hopes. Within a season, virtually every known Spell-caster had become a member of The Guild of The Stone Circle. Azael had accomplished so much in such a short time that he could hardly believe his good fortune.

The scale of the achievement was brought home to him one evening, long after the sun had set. Sitting alone at the top of the hill, he looked down over the standing-stones and their moonlight shadows far below. Beyond, too numerous to count, the cooking-fires of the Spell-casters spangled the thickening night like flickering insects. Azael rose and walked slowly around the blunt summit, looking for some place where the darkness remained unbroken. He could find none; The Henge was completely surrounded by a ring of light which seemed to form a barrier between the hill and advancing night.

The continued success of The Guild brought a crop of problems which Azael had not foreseen. The air was now clear of wasteful and contradictive magickery; the spells of The Guild were discharged with ease and professionalism; and the inhabitants of Krystonia, well pleased with the results achieved by the new regime, brought gifts of food and drink to the wizards as tokens of their gratitude. Unfortunately, they did not bring any Krystal. Most of The Guild's magic was being fired through The Dom, there being few other Krystals available to the enormous, but static, Guild. A hastily organised search of the locality had produced only a small amount, hardly enough to relieve the demands made on The Dom. To compound the problem, Azael was surrounded by a small army of Spell-casters who, quite naturally, wanted to cast spells. They had kept their side of the bargain; now he would have to keep his. But how? Once again, circumstances intervened and worked in Azael's favour.

The Om-ba-Dons, sent by their newly appointed Arch Elder, came to seek a special favour. They could see the wizards were busy, but requested immediate audience with Azael; it was, they stressed, a matter of some urgency. A hot wind from east of the Mountains of Kappah (the Maj-Dron and the Cluod-Hakkom were, as yet, unknown) had, for several days, been assailing their homelands. The wind the Om-ba-Dons could endure; the snow-melt it was causing they could not. Many of their lodges were flooded, some even swept away. They had been advised that The Guild of The Stone Circle were the only ones who might be able to help.

Azael listened sympathetically as the Om-ba-Don messengers unfolded their tale of woe. When they had finished he thought for a while and then explained his position. Much as he understood their plight and wanted to assist, he was afraid he had to refuse. To work a counteracting spell would necessitate much Krystal-power and, with the situation as it was, that was something he could not spare.

Much to Azael's surprise and delight, the Om-ba-Dons divested themselves of their backpacks, extracted two sacks and, with a theatrical flourish, tipped several shining Krystals out at his feet. Their Arch Elder was well aware of the Spell-casters' need for Krystals which, though often seen in the Kappah were never collected, the Om-ba-Don having no use for them. However, if The Guild of The Stone Circle succeeded in driving back the wind from whence it came, the Arch Elder had given his solemn word that the Clans of Om-ba-Don would collect any Krystals they found henceforth and deliver these to The Guild.

Azael, now happily able to accommodate their request, summoned Shoof, explained the problem and let the weather-worker release a spell from The Dom. The result must have been entirely satisfactory for, within days, a train of Om-ba-Dons arrived outside The Henge, each with a heavily laden Gowdan, and unloaded a considerable shipment of Krystal. They assured the wizards on leaving that further supplies would soon follow. And follow they did!

News of this magical favour in return for a gift of Krystal

reached the ears of many others. Representatives from far and wide began to appear with Krystal donations and requests for particular spells to be worked to their advantage. At first, Azael considered all cases on their merits; but such was the eventual demand, there grew a long backlog of requests beseeching The Guild to perform spells which ranged from averting some natural catastrophy to curing a minor affliction, no matter how many Krystals were brought, The Guild needed more and more, the shortfall in power being compensated for by The Dom. And still the queue of Spell-casters waiting to use it grew ever longer; it was soon discharging spell after spell. Azael feared that everything he had worked so hard to accomplish was teetering on the brink of collapse. But The Dom was greater than even he knew.

On one of the rare occasions when he personally undertook the working of a spell, Azael witnessed a strange phenomenon. He placed the Krystal he was preparing to use on top of The Dom while thumbing through a spellbook, searching for details of his intended incantation. Having found the appropriate instructions, he took the smaller Krystal, held it up, spoke the words and waited . . . Nothing happened! The Krystal refused to respond, behaving like one whose powers were long since spent. Azael might have attributed this to some confusion in the rotation of The Guild's small Krystal stock, or to a less than honest client, had he not noticed the brightly glowing patch on the surface of The Dom where, moments earlier, the small Krystal had rested. He ordered a replacement and repeated the process. Again, the new Krystal caused a patch of light to appear on the Dom's surface and, afterwards, failed to release any power of its own. He could hardly believe his luck. The Dom Krystal, unlike any other, appeared capable of recharging itself by absorbing the powers within lesser stones! If enough

Krystals could be found with which to replenish The Dom, its power would be inexhaustible!

Such a timely discovery secured Azael's unopposed re-election as the leader of The Guild of The Stone Circle for another year-term. It was as well; he was about to embark upon the final stages of his revolutionary programme of change.

The changes initiated by Azael had done much to improve the quality of magic-making and the relationship between the Spell-casters and the other inhabitants of Krystonia. But still more changes would be needed if he were to achieve something which would endure. The raw material of his vision he had collected; now he needed to lay sound foundations upon which future generations could build and improve.

The knowledge of individual Guild members varied considerably; some were skilled in many areas whilst others specialised in just one. A few of the younger magicians had knowledge of but a single incantation or spell. It was clear that this imbalance needed to be rectified, but The Guild had become so extensive that Azael could not possibly supervise every spell personally, particularly where very advanced magic was involved. Having enjoyed little opportunity to pursue his own education since the day the two Wendlock Wizards had agreed to follow his leadership, he had become increasingly aware that, compared to many of those he now directed, his magical skill was woefully undeveloped. Azael's solution was to form the Council of Wizards.

With great care he selected thirty Spell-casters from the ranks of The Guild whom he believed would form a responsible and effective body. These would be his Council. Some, such a Magon, Gilbran and Shoof were natural choices, having proved themselves more than adept at using the power of The Dom effectively and well disposed to suggesting improvements. The remainder, Azael picked by evaluating the contents of their spellbooks, concentrating particularly on those who showed outstanding knowledge in some specialised field of magickery.

Between them, the thirty members of The Council began the difficult task of assessing the ability of every single member of The Guild, assigning each a specific title or rank which reflected his or her degree of proficiency. The most highly skilled were a small group known as the Master Wizards, from whose ranks future Council members would be chosen. Next, a larger group of Dom Wizards who had shown themselves to be capable of shaping and controlling a spell through The Dom Krystal, but who had not yet developed seven spells of their own design. Lastly the Apprentices; these were sub divided into the Novices and the True Apprentices. To become a Novice required only a demonstration of the most elementary magical knowledge and aptitude which, after a period of extensive training, would lead to the title of True Apprentice. There would follow a much longer and extremely detailed course under the close supervision of a Master Wizard which, once several challenging examinations had been passed, would lead to the rank of Dom Wizard.

As Azael had expected, there was some argument over who should and who should not be placed in this, that or the other category. Yet even he was suprised how readily The Guild embraced the idea. He was even more surprised, its members welcomed The Council's first ever decree; whereas in the past, the contents of a Spell-caster's spellbook had been a jealously guarded secret, it would henceforth be pooled and made freely available to all! They realised it would now be possible for them to gain the widest knowledge their development required and to attain much greater proficiency and credibility by paying closer attention to their magic-making.

With the day to day running of The Guild now entrusted to The Council, Azael was able to spend a little time practising his own magic and, more importantly, plan the finishing touches which would tie all The Guild's operations together.

It seemed to him that great savings on Krystal-power could be made if spells required by the more distant settlements could be performed on the spot, rather than using a significant amount of magical energy in projecting them all the way from The Henge. Having dispossessed these settlements of their local Magicians in the first place, Azael saw it as his duty to reinstate them. But these would not be unskilled amateurs; they would be Master Wizards, responsible for a small professional team of Dom Wizards and Apprentices who would work together to service the magical requirements of an entire area. Of course, regular reports would have to be made to The Council at The Henge, who would in turn supply provisions, information and advice. The magicians thus placed would remain in post for a predetermined period of what Azael termed service 'in the field', before being recalled to The Henge to write up detailed reports, train, and pursue their further studies; their vacated posts would, meanwhile, be filled by suitable replacements.

But where would all this training and documentation take place? It was bad enough already with spellbooks and incantation recipes stacked in untidy piles in this shelter and that. Trying to find anything required much patience and perseverence; going from one wizard to the one he claimed to whom he had lent the spell, who could not remember having borrowed it in the first place and so on, back to the beginning, was not an uncommon occurrence! Such chaos annoyed Azael who, you will recollect, liked everything neatly arranged. In his experience, ordered paperwork was a prerequisite of orderly magic-making. Would he have tracked down The Dom had his diaries not been so meticulously kept? if details of a successful spell were always ready to hand, there would be no cause for it to ever mis-fire. Such spells as did go wrong should also be catalogued, so that they might be improved upon until they yielded a satisfactory outcome. And the Apprentices: they would need instruction in keeping spellbooks to a high standard of presentation, and be made to practice their hand-script until it was consistently neat and legible. All this needed to be done. But how? And where? Azael had the strangest feeling the solution was already down to him but, try as he might, he could not think what it was. The necessary reminder was not long in coming.

Agoras was a strange character. He rarely mixed socially with the other Guild members, showed little interest in magic, and spent most of his time inside his shelter on an outermost edge of the encampment. His home reflected his only real pleasure in life — building. It was a solid, serviceable cabin with wooden floor, slate roof, fireplace and snugly-fitting shutters. Compared to the ramshackle branch-and-earth dwellings of his peers, it was positively palatial.

One morning, he had approached Azael requesting to be granted a few moments of his time. He had something in his possession which only Azael should see. Welcoming the opportunity of conversing with this reclusive member of The Guild, Azael invited Agoras to visit him in his own shelter, inwardly smiling at the old wizard's critical appraisal of its primitive design and construction.

For a while, Azael was content to make small talk but, after discovering Agoras's fondness for one-word replies followed by uneasy silences, he had finally enquired directly as to his reason for wanting to see him.

Agoras fumbled inside his tunic, produced an old-looking scroll of parchment and sat cradling it protectively. "I have discovered this amongst my drawings. It was not there before and is not in my hand; though I wish with all my heart it were."

"What is it?" enquired Azael.

"An architectural draft."

"Of what?"

"A building."

"Yes of course," sighed Azael, somewhat disappointed. He had hoped it might have been details of some ancient unknown spell. "What sort of building?"

"A kind of Obelisk I think."

"What? An Obber-what?"

"Obelisk; though way beyond the capabilities of any mind known to me. It is . . . in . . . incredible! I cannot imagine what or who could have . . ." As Agora's voice trailed off, he sat staring at the scroll, finding it hard to make further explanation. "I confess," he said at length "that I am jealous."

"Come now, Agoras. You do not expect me to believe that some Apprentice has produced a drawing which so impresses you?"

"No!" Agoras exclaimed vehemently. "This is the work of no Apprentice alive! This is the work of someone . . . some-one . . ."

"Someone . . ?"

"Greater than you or I or The Council, Greater than anyone."

'Heavens!' thought Azael. 'I fear old Agoras has spent too long alone in his cabin'. He coughed and regarded the old wizard sympathetically. "And why is this . . . err . . . obelisk of such importance to you?"

"Because I must build it."

"So why come to me? You know more of these matters than any other member of The Guild. If it pleases you, then build it." Azael smiled; perhaps his reassurance would sweeten Agoras's obvious discomfort.

"Here on this hill, inside The Henge of Oria; this is where I must build!" Agoras said, all in a rush.

Azael's eyes shot wide open in disbelief. "What?"

"It must stand here. I know it!"

"No, Agoras," said Azael, his voice hardening in tone, "build what you will where you will, but do not even consider . . ."

"It is you who should consider, Azael Stormslayer," Agoras imposed. "It is you who should consider this!" He unfastened the scroll and spread it out on the floor.

Azael stared blankly at the parchment, straining to compose himself. The old wizard seemed deadly serious. How was he to make his position clear without resorting to strong or hurtful words?

"As you can see, there are thirty layers each to fit upon the other, rising up into this central obelisk of similar, though eminently superior, design to those adopting The Interlocking Principle of . . ."

Agora's explanation was wasted. All Azael saw were his hands, moving back and forth across the parchment. At once he recalled a dream of many seasons past; could those hands be the same? "Agoras, have you ever set eyes on me before?" he enquired, uncertain of how to begin.

"What do you mean?" asked Agoras, eyes fixed upon the parchment. "Before when?"

"Before you came to The Henge."

"Yes. I believe so."

"Where?"

"In a dream. You called out and said . . . Oh, this is preposterous. It was only a dream."

"Please. It is important. What did I call out?"

"You were shouting at me, 'I don't understand! I don't

understand!'"

"So it was you Agoras! They were your hands I saw! Your hands! This parchment!"

"Now I do not understand," wondered Agoras. "You say me?"

"Yes! Well, your hands at least. And this!" Azael pointed at the parchment. "Do you know what it is?"

"Yes. I have told you. It's an obelisk."

"No! It is more! Far more! It is everything! Can you really build it?"

"I believe I have no choice. I must, even if I have to lay each stone myself."

"Build it you shall, we shall, everyone shall!" Azael was ecstatic. "What is the building named according to the plan?"

"The Krystellate Obelisk."

"The last piece of my vision. The end and beginning of everything. We shall build The Krystellate Obelisk!"

Azael no longer harboured any doubts that forces beyond his understanding had been working through him; Agoras, of course, shared the same belief. The Council, whilst unnerved by the scale of the undertaking they proposed, had to concede there had been too many coincidences for everything to have fallen so perfectly in place without some prior plan.

The building would be colossal. Twenty-nine layers, each slightly smaller than the last, built from interlocking blocks of granite of the type the Om-ba-Don call 'snow-fire rock', alluding to its crystalline structure which produces a flash and dazzle similar to fresh snow in bright sunlight. The thirtieth level, a soaring tower with a pyramidal apex, would be built of the same stone to support, upon a dais at its pinnacle, the huge Dom Krystal. The tower would be entered through a single metal-banded door, leading on to a

spiral staircase of seven hundred and seventy-seven steps —
the only means of access to the dais and The Dom.

The parchment in Agora's custodianship showed the
internal appointments of the lower twenty-nine layers to be
everything and more that Azael could have wished.
Incorporated in the design were conference chambers,
lecture rooms, private dwelling quarters, study bedrooms,
sculleries, kitchens, pantries, workshops, laboratories and,
most importantly of all, a huge space on the second level
designated a library, large enough to accommodate the
collected spellbooks, magical recipes, incantations,
parchments, documents and reports of The Guild and still
leave ample space to store the knowledge of untold
generations of Spell-casters yet to come.

The Guild gave their wholehearted support to the
ambitious project and were quick to come forward and offer
their assistance with its construction, no doubt aware that
the sooner the Obelisk was a reality, the sooner they would
have somewhere safe and secure in which to live. But, as
Agoras himself remarked, one glance at the magicians'
homes revealed how little practical help they would be. The
minds of most Spell-casters, whilst quite able to grasp the
subtleties involved in calculating the impact power of an
incantation, seemed to go blank when confronted by a
problem involving solid objects. Their hands were too soft to
labour long and, even if they proved to be not entirely useless
— which Agoras seriously doubted — they were too few in
number to make much impression; the task would take a
hundred seasons or more to complete. Some members of
The Council did suggest he scaled down the building to a
more manageable size. His reply does not bear my
repeating; suffice it to say, the idea was not put to him twice.
Agoras was going to build the Obelisk as it was meant to be
built. There would be no shortcuts or half-measures.

Azael's answer to the labour shortage was to send out

messengers who travelled far and wide, inviting all the inhabitants of Krystonia, no matter what their race or creed, to meet after winter at the Henge of Oria on the seventh day of The Reawakening.

When the day at last arrived, Azael was staggered by the response. From the Mountains of Kappah came a representation of Om-ba-Don two thousand strong, each with a giggling Boboll riding upon his Gowdan pack-animal's back. Dragons, young and old, winged and Grumblypeg came from Cairn-Tor. A contingent appeared from each settlement and those Gadozorri who could be spared from their seafaring duties had put aside their dislike of dry land and travelled many days to reach the Henge at the appointed time. Most numerous of all, to Agoras's delight, a host of swarthy-featured Trolles journeyed from the Forest of Keldorran armed with an assortment of spades, picks and other useful tools. At noon on that seventh day of Reawakening, the most momentous meeting in Krystonia's past took place. Azael ascended a small platform specially erected on top of the hill and, looking down at the patchwork field of faces gathered together inside The Henge, he spoke in loud and clear voice of his vision; of The Great Design:-

"If all of you assembled will agree to assist in the building of the Obelisk and, upon its completion, promise to deliver every Krystal you find to the Spell-casters, I will swear a binding oath. Help, advice, education, shelter and healing will be everyone's for the asking. None will go hungry, and the Three Seasons will come and go without interruption for the rest of time. The Obelisk will serve as a reminder to all of our agreement. From this day forth, you can all become part of the same Great Design!"

Azael's speech was greeted with a tumultuous ovation. He had succeeded not only in bringing the Spell-casters together but, now, virtually every known Krystonian race. Yet there were those who having watched unseen, turned back to the Waste of Shugg with coldness in their hearts. They would, much later, prove to have ambitious designs of their own!

And so the Krystellate Obelisk came to be built on the hilltop, enclosed by The Henge of Oria. The Om-ba-Don quarried and hauled massive blocks of granite from the Kappah; the dragons fetched and carried for Agoras and flew reconnaissance missions in search of desired materials; the Bobolls 'popped' back and forth, delivering messages and collecting together equipment; the Gadazorri males steamed timbers into shape whilst the females spun fabric and embroidered tapestries which could adorn every room upon completion; the settlement-dwellers worked from sunrise to sunset without complaint, erecting scaffolding and braiding ropes; the Spell-casters cooked, tended and administered to the ailing; and the Trolles . . . the Trolles did everything! Agoras is reputed to have said: "Give me a mountain of rock, a forest of trees and an army of Trolles and I'll build you a house for everyone in Krystonia within a season!"

He could not have been serious, for the Obelisk itself took six seasons to build. The Tower, its central core, was raised up layer by layer beneath the pyramidal apex on which The Dom was set. Higher and higher it rose until, on the twenty-eighth day of Harvest, Azael and Agoras jointly, emplaced the last stone. The huge monolith which, by Agora's calculation, stood two hundred and twenty-one wizard-paces tall, shone white in the light of the sun, glowed pale by the light of both moons, and held up The Dom for the surrounding lands to see. It was, and still is now, an incredible sight. The final link was complete and the Great Design set in motion!

The wizards trained hard, underwent stringent examinations and went out to discharge their duties and good works amongst the settlements. The library grew apace, eventually necessitating the appointment of Zanohn as the first of the Librarians, who began the unenviable task of sifting and sorting, restoring and, finally, indexing the collected written material of The Guild of The Stone Circle. Krystals were delivered regularly by representatives of the various races; and the dragons initiated the first transportation treaty. Season came and season went without upset or drastic occurrence and, ere the long winter descended, all Spell-casters returned to the Obelisk to study and further improve their Art. The power of The Dom united them all.

Agoras, unwilling to spend time practising magickery when he could be planning and building, left to dwell with the Trolles in the Forest of Keldorran, hoping he might improve their ability to interpret architectural drafts. His success, it transpired, was limited. The Trolles would follow his directions to the letter when he were present to supervise them but, if left alone with a set of drawings and the required materials, the outcome would always be a bridge! Whilst eager to do his bidding, they found it impossible to work on their own initiative; the 'Three-toed Bridge-Building Trolle' side of their personalities always seeming to come to the fore. Still, Agoras and his Trolles did bequeath a wealth of fine bridges to Krystonia, spanning streams, rivers, narrow gorges and wide ravines; though the only purpose some seemed to serve, out in the middle of nowhere, was in providing the industrious Trolles with their brand of ideal home! "Show me a bridge and I'll show you a bagful of Trolles asleep beneath it!" is another of Agoras's many oft-quoted sayings.

However, the Trolle females, who show none of their spouses' hankering to dwell beneath bridges, were extremely grateful for Agoras's insistence that the errant husbands should build under his watchful eye, the terraces of snug cottages in which nearly all Trolles dwell today.

Stoope Dragon — sits the youngster Owhey and the newest-born, Tokkel.

(Though, it must be said, the husbands frequently make excuses about taking junior for a walk and then nip away to build bridges with their friends!)

Azael Stormslayer presided for many more seasons to come at the head of The Council of Wizards, who steadfastly refused to let him retire and make way for a more youthful replacement. His beard grew to a length only bettered by the venerable Gilbran and, like all who followed in his footsteps as custodians of the Obelisk, he was formally addressed as The Doyen of The Guild of the Stone Circle. His work was complete, his vision a reality, yet still he continued to work upon the development of his magical skills and make detailed entries in his fifty-second spell-diary. The last entry, long since committed to the Obelisk's archives, provides the only reliable clue to his mysterious disappearance one morning on the seventh day of The Reawakening. At the foot of the page, in his script, are written the words, "I GO WITH ORIA." Some Apprentices, receiving instruction inside The Henge were the last to claim to have seen him. He was, they insisted even after close interrogation, seated upon the grass, sharing a loaf with some old woman whose face was unfamiliar but which Azael appeared to know well.

When first I accepted the post of Recorder, The Council generously furnished me with private chambers on the third level of the Obelisk; comfortable well-appointed rooms they were, complete with a small balcony overlooking the library. The arrangement was very convenient. Parchments, scrolls and documents requiring my translation were close to hand and my meals, chosen from a small but well-balanced menu, I could eat in one of the communal refectories or have brought directly to my rooms. Despite such a comfortable lifestyle, however, I had approached The Council of Wizards within a season of my residency and persuaded them to allow me to move out to the Forest of Keldorran, there to continue my work. I did not wish to appear ungrateful, but I simply could not bear the hustle and bustle and the interminable questions of the Apprentices who appeared to view me as a veritable source of information. Now, though I must cater for my own needs, I can sleep, eat and work when I please. It is far easier for me to apply myself to my tasks with only the sound of the forest creatures and the voice of the wind for company.

Reammon, the Librarian of the Obelisk, is completely opposite in his nature. He positively thrives on the busy atmosphere and the pressures involved in the library's administration. Under his direction, a new system of index cards has recently been introduced which allows specific information to be found quickly and with ease. Not that Reammon himself needs such an aid; his powers of recall are prodigious. After only a few moments consideration he can usually name the shelf number, volume number and, not infrequently, the exact page number of an entry. The Apprentices, never ones to waste time pursuing anything as mundane as a reference spell, ask Reammon sooner than use his index system. I have often thought he must know more spell-words and incantations than the majority of the Master Wizards, such is the extent of his knowledge.

Our work is closely linked. I translate all parchments into Common-tongue and, through my researches, place them in a chronological order so that a clearer, more comprehensive picture of our history might be passed on for the enlightenment of future Krystonians. Reammon takes these translations, has copies made by the Obelisk scribes and sees that they are bound into volumes, numbered and placed on the appropriate shelves. At least once every season I go to the Obelisk, meet with Reammon and discuss recent discoveries; then we schedule our work, exchange information and consider new projects. It may interest you to know that it was Reammon who proposed these writings. He thought it might be a rewarding task for me to set down a personal account of the present life of Krystonians and something of our past in a way which would appeal to the general reader. I am aware that this involves much background description and only hints at the wealth of tales and experiences surrounding characters and events; but, given time and continued health, these will surely follow.

Besides myself and those wizards on placements in the settlements, there are others whose lives centre upon the Obelisk but live some distance from its walls. More often than not, as with Shepf and Rueggan, this is for practical reasons rather than simply a matter of choice.

Rueggan began his career as in inventor in the Obelisk's workshops under the guidance of the Master Wizard, Darphon. He was an outstanding pupil and even before achieving his Dom-Wizard's certificate, was given his own study. It was then that things began to go wrong. The sleeping Spell-casters would have their dreams interrupted by midnight bangs, clanks and floor-shaking explosions as yet another of Rueggan's ambitious projects disappeared in a cloud of smoke! Given frequent tickings-off, he made many promises to modify his conduct and confine his research to more sociable hours, before going back to his room and starting all over again. His experiments grew in scale, as did the accompanying explosion whenever one went awry: The Council became seriously worried that he might one day succeed in blowing the Obelisk assunder. Coupled with this, his collection of ancient machinery grew apace, and it came to light that many of the Apprentices were denied access to their dormitories by the piles of mechancial odds and ends which Rueggan had persuaded them to store on his behalf. Then there were the Gorphs. Unbeknown to anyone, Rueggan had housed a small army of these little creatures in his room and, one night whilst his concentration was focussed on applying the finishing touches to his latest creation, they slipped out and went exploring. Their subsequent re-organisation of the library did not endear them to Reammon!

It was the last straw. Rueggan, his mountain of scrap metal and the Gorphs were transferred to a cavern in the Valley of Wendlock, where he works to this day. Darphon has long since gone and Rueggan assumed his position. However, even though now a respected and influential member of The Council, he only visits the Obelisk to instruct Apprentices and attend official meetings. The faithful Gorphs, who stick close on his heels and shadow his every move, are kept occupied outside until he collects them. Some of the Apprentices still tease Reammon by shouting: "I say! There's a Gorph loose in the library!" It is said he immediately turns an unusual shade of purple.

I personally think Rueggan revels in his reputation as an eccentric, though I am first to admit he takes his work very seriously. One only has to look at the care and attention he has invested in the Museum of Antiquity located in the Obelisk. It is full of strange and mysterious machines of The Ancients which he has painstakingly restored to working order.

Shepf is a direct descendant of Shoof, the renowned weather-worker of Wendlock and founder member of The Guild of The Stone Circle. He inhabits a magnificent tower, built upon the site of his illustrious ancestor's humble shelter, which boasts hot and cold water, air-conditioning and a lift to save climbing up several flights of stairs. All of these features are powered by a series of windmills installed by Rueggan and turned by breezes summoned by Shepf himself — for Shepf is Krystonia's foremost exponent of the Art of Wind-Working. High in his tower he works spells to summon light breezes, dispel whirlwinds and hurricanes, and bring hot winds from off the Desert of Cluod-Hakkom to dry the lands after heavy rains. His skill is well developed and he is highly regarded by his colleagues on The Council, the settlement-dwellers and, especially, the birds who rely upon him providing favourable tailwinds to assist their southerly migration at Harvest's end. He and Rueggan, being of similar age and graduating as Master-Wizards in the same year, have always been close friends. In their youth, that friendship almost led to their downfall.

Flying, Shepf was convinced, would not be too difficult to achieve with a suitable pair of wings and correct windspeed. He persuaded Rueggan, who required very little persuading, to make them both the wings, while he would provide the necessary winds to ensure an easy take-off.

The first The Council knew of their scheme was when a howling gale descended upon the Obelisk in the middle of what had previously been a pleasant and tranquil day. Moments later, the two young wizards were sighted high in the air, clinging to delta-shaped frameworks across which Gadazorri sailcloth had been stretched, spiralling earthwards out of control. Had it not been for two dragons effecting a difficult and dangerous mid-air rescue, Shepf and Rueggan would have been dashed to pieces for sure!

Shepf, though older and wiser now, is still youthful in spirit and many Apprentices claim his lectures on Wind-Working and the interpretation of star charts to be among the most entertaining and enthusiastically presented. I believe it was Shepf's habit of directing winds of varying power through the Obelisk in order to enliven his lectures, which led to his tower being commissioned by The Council of Wizards.

The members of The Council, whilst not all working magic as spectacular as Shepf's, are all experts in their fields and make important contributions to the furthering of The Great Design. Wodema, at present the only wizardess occupying a seat upon The Council, has affected all our lives profoundly. Descended from a potion-maker of small reputation, she has increased our knowledge of healing far beyond what it was in Azael's day. I do not believe there is a single leaf, root or bloom for which she has not discovered some medicinal application. Though ostensibly a resident of the Obelisk, she is rarely to be found there, spending most of her time travelling from settlement to settlement, collecting herbs, diagnosing and curing illnesses, and promoting the planting of herb-gardens to provide Krystonians with living medicine chests. Several Trolle females, after attending a course of Wodema's evening classes, have become quite proficient at effecting cures for minor complaints; further classes have been requested by many settlement-wives and one or two female dragons. The Trolle females are now expressing keen interest in an advanced course in herbalism.

Yet no matter how much Wodema educates and others learn, she possesses something which cannot be taught: she has a way about her, a manner, a certain tone of voice and touch of hand which is a comfort in itself, and a warmth which radiates from within. Her most advanced Apprentice, Kyrschen, has something of this inborn magic and already shows great potential. Perhaps someday she will add to the many herbal recipes, medical reports and botanical catalogues which Wodema has endowed and increase our understanding of healing still further.

Healing is not Wodema's only talent. Her knowledge of plants goes beyond recognition of their type and medicinal usage. As she passes amongst them she talks and touches, as though they were thinking, feeling things capable of understanding. Unorthodox as this may seem, since she began to work the Spell of Ripening through The Dom and cause the Fired-Light to fall upon the crops, Krystonia has enjoyed harvests of unprecedented bounty. It is as though the warmth of her heart, her gentle kindness, her love of all things great and small, is captured by the great Krystal and showered upon the land. Many settlement-dwellers claim to know the exact moment every year when Wodema begins to speak into The Dom. They say the birds fall silent, the breeze holds its breath and all noise ceases; as if the whole of Krystonia pauses for a timeless moment and considers the glory and beauty of its being. I know exactly what they mean.

Recently, Wodema has begun working on a combined project with the wizards Rohan and Tador. Together they hope to transform the Steppes of Shimm, on the east side of Kappah, into land capable of producing useful grain crops. Rohan, who has developed several new plant strains, is attempting to culture a hardy, heat and sand resistant type by utilising Krystal power to fuse the tough grass native to the area with chiffan, one of the high-yeilding crops successfully grown on the fertile lowlands.

Tador has been experimenting with samples of sand from the Steppes, investigating the possibility of improving its fertility by the addition of minerals and salts. He has also studied the Om-ba-Don terracing system in detail to see if, somehow, it might be adapted. Whilst his experiments have given promising results, he must still find a way of separating the required minerals from rocks and rain water before devising a method whereby sufficient quantities can be readily transported to the Steppes. Wodema has been sending out bursts of Fired-Light at Tador's request to settle upon this arid region. She is not too hopeful of success, but Tador seems to think that, over a period of time, it may decrease the need for additional fertilizers. Who knows? he may make farmers of the Maj-Dron yet!

In contrast to such practical applications, there are two Master Wizards who work very special magic, of which few before have ever had knowledge.

Turfen, at present The Doyen of The Guild of The Stone Circle, is the only Spell-caster who can consistently use the Dom Krystal and combine its powers with the silver light of

Gos and Ghedra to produce the delicate and diaphanous magic of dreaming. I suspect there may have been an illusionist or two somewhere in his ancestry, but now his skill goes far beyond the realms of simple imagery. He has the power to bring blissful deep restoring sleep to those whose minds are sorely troubled or, if needed, to release the thoughts and desires of the subconscious mind. This latter ability is used very rarely, for Turfen cannot see or experience the images his magic has provoked, only see their effects on an individual. Sometimes, these may be very disturbing. We all, no matter how pure of thought we try to be, have secret thoughts which are better kept locked away.

Like Turfen's, the magic of Haapf is concerned with emotions; but, unlike Turfen, Haapf shows no reticence when it comes to using his talents on others. Ask any members of The Council for a brief assessment of his character and I will guarantee that comments such as 'irresponsible', 'slap-dash' and 'scatterbrained' will feature prominently among the replies. Where Rueggan is mildly eccentric and Shepf is a touch flamboyant, Haapf is downright incorrigible.

He is always late for appointments, rarely writes anything down in his spellbook, fidgets or sleeps through Council meetings, plays practical jokes at inopportune moments, fails to deliver his own scheduled lectures, interrupts those already in progress and encourages a lack of respect for authority amongst the Apprentices. Anyone else behaving in such a manner would have been expelled from the Obelisk long ago. Not so Haapf. Even when other members of The Council have joined forces and taken him to task over his unprofessional attitude, Haapf has quickly won them round and left them smiling and praising his name!

In spite of his multitude of shortcomings, Haapf is universally popular. His magic is that of mirth, smiling and general lightness of heart. I have seen those beset with depression or struck down with illness put on a smile at the sound of his voice. He is like a lighted candle entering a darkened room. There is truly something about him which shines!

It was Haapf's idea for he and Turfen to combine forces and send out spells of pleasant dreams and mirth towards Krak N'Borg in the hope that a sudden change of character in the Snords would bring about the Dark Lord's downfall. It was an enterprising scheme, but the spells appear to have been vigorously rebuffed by either N'Borg or N'Chakk, for Turfen suffered from a series of terrible nightmares shortly afterwards and poor Haapf's face was frozen into a scowl which took several days of incantations to unlock.

To conclude my brief summary of a few of the more illustrious characters associated with the Obelisk, I must make mention of one who many believe holds more sway, commands more respect and deference than The Doyen and The Council put together. He is no Spell-caster but the denizen of the Obelisk's kitchens, the King of the Stew-pots, the terribly tempered swinger of spoons, Hottlepottle!

Hottlepottle, or Hotpot as he is usually called when well out of earshot, is the Obelisk's Head Chef, whose purpose is to provide the residents with meals at regular times. These are always cooked to perfection, well-presented and nutritious; a perfect foil for Hotpot himself who is raw, ruffled and difficult to stomach on some occasions. He is best likened to a kettle with a tightly fitting lid — you never can tell when he is about to explode.

When a meal is well received, when compliments alluding to his gastronomic prowess are forthcoming, when every platter has been cleaned of every last morsel, Hotpot is gregarious, jovial, almost affable. But should his Chief Apprentice, Zygmund, put a pinch too much seasoning in the sauce, should anyone make the most helpful suggestion about a change in the menu or leave a speck of food upon their platter, Hotpot is transformed in a flash.

Purpling with rage he will throw his pots and pans out of their cupboards, smash platters, hurl cutlery, ingredients and insults in equal measure, and pursue the petrified Zygmund around the preparation table, promising to add him to the stew! So fearful are some of the Apprentices, if they cannot eat their way through one of his mountainous meals, they will attempt to shovel the leftovers onto a neighbour's platter or sneak them into their tunic pockets. This is no simple feat, for Hotpot watches over them as they eat. Woe betide any who are caught trying to fool him! Haapf frequently suggests that The Council send their Head Chef to Krak N'Borg. "The Snord Legions," he says, "would sooner desert to the Waste of Shugg than endure Hotpot for more than a day!"

Of course, he is not serious. Without Hottlepottle the Obelisk would loose some of its colour and excitement, and an excellent cook into the bargain. And there is a softer side to his nature, to which he would never openly admit, which lies just beneath his hard exterior. It is easily touched by one small individual in particular.

Grackene, the Trolle-wife, can twist Hotpot around any one of her little fingers. He adores her, reveres her, hangs upon her every word like a lovestruck Apprentice. Zygmund says he has heard Hotpot make proposals of marriage on more than one occasion, actually kneeling down in front of the diminutive Trolle female, beseeching her with all his heart and the promise of shared recipe books! He seems in no way deterred when she scolds him, tells him to stop being so stupid and declares her love for her husband, Groc.

The source of her attraction, it seems, has little to do with personality or her disarming smile, but sponge cakes! Her cooking is always of the highest order, but her sponge cakes excel; they melt in the mouth. Time after time she has patiently taken Hotpot through her recipe, step by careful step, and time after time Hotpot fails to make a single tiny cake which can compare to any of hers. Incredibly, even in the face of such a direct affront to his culinary credibility, he smiles dotingly, pats her head and exclaims, "How lightly your fingers sift the flour! How perfectly you heat the oven! How you honour me with your presence in my humble kitchen!"

I personally prefer Hotpot as the terribly tempered swinger of spoons!

Entrusted as I am with the reporting of events as they occur, I have no choice in the subjects about which I write. I cannot dwell on those which interest me and omit those which do not. Unlike a storyteller, I cannot fabricate intricate plots to heighten the reader's enjoyment; where any unfold on my parchment, they do so because they already belong within the framework of known happenings. I do not relate accounts of gripping adventures unless and until I can establish their source and vouch safe their accuracy. True, I may add a touch of colour here and there and condense many perspectives to produce a clear image, but my portrayals are strictly determined by the bounds or real events and not by the expansiveness of my imagination.

By and large I have found this a most pleasurable occupation, well-suited to one so fond of the written word, but there are occasions when it has been necessary to record those things which touch my heart with sadness and remorse.

All things change with the passing of time. Though we may try to alter its course, or even check its flow, time tolerates no interruption — it passes us by like the river on its way to the sea. Who will speak of me when another sits at my desk? How soon before the name of Kephren the Recorder is known only to those who read my accounts?

I write of such things here for the events which I am about to relate, to draw this First Chronicle to a close, will bring the sorrow of scripting many names for the last time — dear friends who are now part of some Great Design as yet unknown to me.

This then, is my account of the blackest period in the history of Krystonia — the Battle for The Dom!

The Spell-casters observe carefully the cycle of the two moons before issuing the Great Spell from The Dom which unfetters the chains of the cold. After the long nights and twilight days of Winter, the advent of Reawakening is greeted with a sudden flurry of activity as the inhabitants respond to changes in the land on which they depend for their livelihood.

Overnight, the snows begin to melt. The ice on rivers and mountain tarns groans as it recedes, unlocking the waters beneath. Dormant seeds, stirred by the rapidly warming sun thrust the first shoots of green into daylight, while leaf buds swell quickly and unfurl.

There is, at this time, a mood of hope and excitement abroad, throughout the waking land. Windows are unshuttered in the settlements and doors thrown open wide as the inhabitants drive out the stale air of winter and usher in the pure fragrance of fresh life. The Septs of Om-ba-Don tend their terraces and repair ditches, dams and walls which have succumbed to the ravages of winter; the Maj-Dron strike out from Tholgah-Loh to begin a new cycle of the Cluod-Hakkom; the Gadazorri weigh anchor and set sail for the coastal settlement of Torz, once again feeling the heave and yaw of the Rahpans' decks as they put forth from sheltered bays and ride the offshore swell; and the Master Wizards journey from the Krystellate Obelisk with their teams of newly appointed Apprentices and Dom Wizards, to take up their allotted posts among the settlements.

There lately dawned a Reawakening which was not as we have come to expect. Everything appeared to be progressing well, and yet an unmistakable under-current of foreboding seemed part of the air itself. Something was wrong; even the birds seemed to sense it. They showed no inclination to set about building their nests; instead they sat forlornly in the trees, twittering softly to each other as though some secret were passing between them. More and more quiet did they become until, one morning, I found them gone, flown away in the night. The Forest of Keldorran fell silent.

The weather maintained a slow but steady improvement for a while, but then took a sudden unseasonal turn for the worse; life's well-established pattern showed signs of breaking down and the resources of The Council of Wizards were stretched to unprecedented levels. Much worse was to follow.

The season of Growth, marked as a rule by long hot days and showers of soft refreshing overnight rain, became a season of torrential downpour and terrifying electrical storms. Heavy skies were split by zigzag trails of white lightning; trees were cleaved in two or transformed into charcoal shells; croplands lay flattened and scarred by the erosive force of running water; terraces collapsed, dams were breached and the sodden topsoil of whole meadows was washed away. The River Cauld, with its many tributaries, flowed brown and swollen.

The pressures on teams of outposted Spell-casters were constant, and their demands upon Krystal stocks began to outstrip supply. Only The Dom, throwing out counteracting spells by day and by night, brought any respite to the inhabitants of the ravaged settlements. Yet for how long The Council of Wizards could continue to sap The Dom's power before it too faded and left Krystonia at the mercy of the elements, no one really knew. The wizards' appeals for more Krystals to be delivered to the Obelisk met with little response; everyone was far too busy repairing the damage and striving to ensure there would at least be something to harvest which would see them through the lean times of winter.

Desperate situations may need drastic remedies; this one certainly did. After hurried discussion The Council, through Turfen, latest in the long line of Doyens of The

Guild of the Stone Circle, sent Graffyn to approach the dragons of Cairn Tor and ask for their assistance.

Grunch was, of course, fully aware of the circumstances surrounding his visit. Business had been severely disrupted by the weather and he was faced with a growing backlog of commissions which, he feared, might not be honoured if the storms continued to play havoc with his schedules. Thus when Graffyn arrived at Cairn Tor, the dragon was not in the best of vapours; the wizard was subjected to an exhaustive list of complaints alluding to the Spell-casters' shortcomings before he could put their request to Dragon Transport Limited's Chief Executive.

"The Council beseeches you to release two winged dragons from all their other duties," Graffyn began at last, "and send them at once to the Obelisk. There they will be fitted with spell-charged Krystals, to ward off the extremes of cold and blistering heat they will encounter on their mission . . ."

"What mission?" inquired Grunch.

"Give me chance and I will tell you! They are to fly over the Kappah and across the Desert of Cluod-Hakkom in search of the tribes of the Maj-Dron. Having found them, they are to relay a vital message to Shigger, their head chieftain . . ."

"What message?"

". . . Requesting that he and his people abandon their trek to the mining grounds and return to Tholgah-Loh, laden with Krystal. Your dragons would, of course, be told all this at the Obelisk but, I suppose, you do have a right to know. Om-ba-Don couriers will await their arrival at Tholgah-Loh to relieve them of the Krystal, in exchange for the provisions they will need to survive such a major disruption in the pattern of their lives. By then, of course, your dragons would long since be back home. I must stress how urgent and crucial is your cooperation!"

Kazahk of the Gadazorri prepares to set sail.

Grunch made no immediate reply but sat regarding the wizard, two plumes of grey smoke issuing from his nose.

"Out of the question," he finally responded. "I've already asked those who can cope with the workload to put in double shifts!"

"You have, I believe, no choice if the Great Design is to continue," said Graffyn resignedly.

"It's that serious?"

Graffyn slowly nodded. "It's that serious."

There followed a long and uncomfortable silence during which Grunch shuffled around the cave, deep in thought, smoke still rising from his nostrils. "Why two dragons?" he asked at length, slumping in front of Graffyn.

"Two would have more chance of success."

"But two might be lost instead of one."

"It's possible," admitted Graffyn.

"Over the Kappah? Over the Cluod-Hakkom? . . ." Grunch looked out of the cavern mouth, away to where another storm growled ominously over the cowering trees of Keldorran, momentarily illuminating the forest with flashes of electric light. "I will ask them," he said quietly, "but we must abide by their decision if they refuse."

"I understand."

It speaks volumes for the dependability of the winged dragons that every single one, young and old, inexperienced and seasoned alike, volunteered his or her services freely. And it says equally as much for Grunch's commitment to the Great Design that he chose his two most trusted fliers at a time when, more than ever, he needed them himself.

Next morning the winged dragons, Groosh and Nimbo, flew from Cairn Tor to the Krystellate Obelisk. Briefed by the wizards whilst the protective Krystals were hung around their necks, they departed without delay, carrying with them The Council's earnest hopes.

Tulan rested his elbows upon a wooden anchor-capstan, cupped his chin in his hands and pensively studied the coastline. Between the waiting flotilla of Rahpans and the shore, the sea heaved storm-grey and restless. Wave after wave rocked the ships and rolled relentlessly landward, to join the ranks of spume-flecked breakers battering the beach, beyond which lay Sobul.

No settlement dwellers appeared from their houses to bring baskets of goods to the shore. Facing directly into the wind and driving rain, it lay deserted of all forms of life, save for a tattered fringe of seaweed strewn upon the sand, which marked the furthest reach of some enormous wave. The tide, Tulan noticed, was on the ebb.

"Do we drop anchor, Captain?"

Tulan glanced at Krellick, his first mate, and then looked back at Sobul, bleak and uninviting. "Yes," he said and nothing more. He stood apart from the rest of his crew as the capstan was unpinned and the stone anchor splashed into the sea.

"Do I tell the trader crews to stand ready, Captain?"

"No; there will be no trade here today, but I shall land and speak with the Fugleman."

"You will ask him for fruit?"

"I will ask."

"Supplies are low. If we do not fill the lockers soon it will only be a matter of time before The Sickness . . ."

"I will ask," Tulan reiterated, "but I do not hold out much hope."

The mate gave the crew their orders and Tulan gazed shoreward once more. He was deeply concerned; trade had suffered badly throughout the freak weather and, whilst the Gadazorri could survive well enough without spices or fibres, they relied upon a continuous supply of fresh fruit for a healthy diet. What had gone wrong? Surely the Spell-casters were aware of the situation? Perhaps the Fugleman of Sobul would know something?

"Ready Captain!"

The shout broke Tulan's thoughts and he strode over to where a boarding net had been draped over the Rahpan's side. Below, bobbing gently in the small patch of calm in the mother ship's lee, a trading boat lay waiting, secured to cleats on the gunwale.

"Signal the other ships. Tell them to make fast and await my return. No point in more than one boat going ashore." Tulan grabbed hold of the net and climbed overboard, his descent cut short by a voice close to his shoulder.

"Careful my son," It was Tallac. "Watch the breakers. I've never seen them so high off Sobul before."

"I'm in good hands father," Tulan replied, motioning towards the six barrel-chested oarsmen already positioned below. "Besides, I would be no wetter if I swam." There was little humour in his voice.

Landward progress was painfully slow. Tallac watched anxiously as the tiny boat rose high for a brief moment and fell back into a seething trough for what seemed an eternity. He held his breath involuntarily each time the little craft vanished, exhaling only when he saw it again, riding the back of the next wave.

Ankles and knees jammed tight against the bulwarks behind the upturned prow, Tulan encouraged his oarsmen who obliged, pulling hard and deep. When close enough to the shelving coast for the towering waves' forward drive to outweigh the tow of the outgoing tide, they began to make faster headway.

The buildings of Sobul slowly assumed their distinctive shapes: squat rows of windowless store houses; open-sided drying sheds; conical smoke houses, each with a tall straight flue; workshops; the dwelling houses of the inhabitants with their red-stone walls and roofs of thatch. Tulan could see them all now, but nowhere a sign of life. Was this the bustling vibrant settlement he had known for as long as he had been tall enough to peek over the guard-rail of his father's Rahpan? Where was everyone? The fleet's arrival was surely expected and, though the weather was foul, it seemed most odd that not even a small gathering waited to greet them from the shore.

Tulan studied the swell. To a Gadazorri seaman, no two waves are alike; some run faster, others break too soon. In such a troubled sea, it was vital he chose the right wave to take them ashore. If he chose well and the oarsmen rowed to perfection, their light little boat would be carried smoothly along on the face of the collapsing wave. But choose incorrectly, row just too fast or too slow and they would be swallowed by the next incoming breaker.

At Tulan's signalled command, the oarsmen began to row furiously. They felt the leading edge of his chosen wave make contact with the boat and gently lift its stern; then the main mass overtook them. They held on grimly as their vessel tilted forward at an acute angle and rode the roaring wall of water. It carried them to the shore as if they were driftwood, and broke about them as their bows scraped gratefully against coarse sand. Hurriedly shipping the oars, they dragged the boat high up the beach, beyond the tidemark of seaweed.

"Well pulled," Tulan commended his oarsmen.

"It was down to your timing, Captain," one of them responded. "Though it will not be so easy getting back!"

"True enough," agreed Tulan, "but let us worry about that later. Now we must find out what has become of the fruit traders of Sobul."

With a wave of their hands towards anxious faces aboard their Rahpan out in the bay, the seven Gadazorri seamen approached the silent settlement.

"I don't like it," sighed Rohan, stroking his beard thoughtfully and drumming his fingers on the richly carved arm of his chair. "Something's happened to him, I'm certain."

"Has he ever been late before?" enquired Turfen.

"You don't know Gwillum like I do! It takes me all my time to persuade him to go to Wendlock to find samples of grass for my research. He was most put out because I sent him off to Keldorran."

The wizard's conversation was interrupted when Haapf, laughing loudly, burst through the door of The Council Chamber. "Ho! Ho! You should have seen his face when it exploded!"

"Whose face?" asked Turfen.

"Why, Hotpot's of course! I put some Expanding Dust in his pudding mixture when he wasn't looking."

"Haapf!" exclaimed Turfen, his voice only slightly reproachful. "You shouldn't do things like that, you really shouldn't."

"Why ever not? Someone's got to brighten things up a bit round here. Look at you two, sitting about with faces sour enough to turn milk into cheese. Is something amiss?"

"It's Gwillum," answered Rohan. "He's not returned from Keldorran."

"Neither have the trees," Haapf let out obtusely, "and I'm not saddened one jot. They can look after themselves and so, I expect, can Gwillum."

"What are you twittering about?" asked Rohan. "He's three whole days overdue !"

"It's no laughing matter," fumed Rohan. Something is wrong; mark my words!"

"He could have taken shelter," offered Turfen. "It hasn't stopped raining for two days at least. Maybe he's found a cave somewhere or a hole up in a hollow tree."

"Not Gwillum!" retorted Rohan. "He'd walk through

snowdrifts rather than miss one hot meal more than he had to. I know something's wrong. I just know it!"

"What do you suggest we do?"

"Let me go and look for him."

"I'm sorry, Rohan, but you know that's out of the question; you can't be spared from the Obelisk. If Shepf and Rueggan are right, and I've a sneaking suspicion they are, then N'Borg is doing his utmost to wear us down."

"Why?"

"Who can say?" Turfen shrugged.

"He's doing a good job of it," said Haapf with uncharacteristic gravity.

"I fear I must agree," replied Turfen. "It would be for the best if none outside The Council were yet made aware of our thoughts. No sense in causing alarm, especially when we can't be sure."

"But what's to be done about Gwillum?" asked Rohan. "Nothing?"

"Wait and see if he returns. If he's still not back in two more days, I'll get some of the Trolles to go and find him. Don't worry; he's bound to be alright."

Rueggan entered the chamber and found the three wizards sitting in silence, lost in their personal thoughts. "Look out everyone; he's after blood!" the newcomer boomed. "And I think I know whose blood it is he's after!"

"What! Who?"

"Hotpot! He's in a towering rage. Claims someone has sabotaged his pudding," said Rueggan, giving Haapf a sideways glance. "I wonder who would do such a thing?"

"Where was he when you last saw him?" asked Haapf, shuffling in his seat and looking positively unsettled.

"Heading right this way!"

"Zounds!" said Haapf, springing to his feet. "He'll boil me alive! You must excuse me; I've just remembered a very important spell recipe I must attend to. If anyone should ask, I'm not to be disturbed." With that, he scurried to the door, checked that the coast was clear outside and disappeared.

His fellow-wizards hooted with laughter and, for a few happy moments, their thoughts were untroubled.

"Poor old Haapf," giggled Turfen. "He's really in a stew!"

"Don't you mean hot water?" chortled Rueggan.

A loud knock on the chamber door broke into their amusement. Turfen opened the door to find an Apprentice bearing a note.

"Please Sir, Shepf has told me to give you this. He says hang onto your hats, whatever that might mean."

Turfen thanked the messenger and, as he read the note, all his tensions and tribulations reasserted themselves. He handed the note to Rohan.

"It looks like we shall have to work again tonight," Rohan said grimly.

"I think it's time we called an emergency meeting of The Council," said Rueggan, who had read the message over Rohan's shoulder." I fear we cannot delay any longer!"

By the time the thirty-strong Council of Wizards had gathered behind closed doors, the storm which Shepf had first seen over Keldorran, was approaching the Henge of Oria.

The trees encircling the Obelisk seemed to shiver to their roots as a strong breeze, running before the main body of the tempest, funnelled through them. It was bitterly cold, carrying on its breath the threat of returning winter from the icy Waste of Shugg, a harbinger of the worst weather yet to challenge The Guild of The Stone Circle's powers. It rapidly swelled to a gale which smashed into the trees, twisting their branches and stripping their leaves before it, touching their sleet-soaked trunks with mantles of rime.

Then came the hail; every living creature ran for shelter as the stinging spheres of ice rattled through the beleaguered branches, pelted the dwellings in the nearby settlements and lashed the very walls of the Obelisk.

The influence of N'Borg could no longer be denied. All Shepf's efforts to divert the path of the storm came to nought and, as he was quick to point out to his colleagues, it had to be driven by powerful magic. It settled over the Obelisk and showed no sign of moving on.

"Well what are we to do, my dears?" asked Wodema. "We can't just sit here and hope it will go away, can we?"

"Can we move it, Shepf?" enquired Turfen.

"We can. But great power will be needed to do so. If we take no action, however, it is N'Borg's power and not ours which is squandered. Why not sit it out and let him exhaust himself?"

"What? Surely you jest!" exclaimed Rohan. "The terraces of the Om-ba-Don are being washed away, the croplands are mostly laid waste and you propose we do nothing! What shall we harvest? What do we say when winter comes and the storehouses stand empty?"

"He's really got it in for us this time," said Rueggan sardonically. "If we take action, we are weakened; if we don't . . . as Rohan says, we starve. And I'm sure we've not seen the worst of it yet."

"What do you mean?" asked Haapf.

"It's obvious N'Borg may be many things but one thing he's not is stupid. He would hardly waste his power for no reason. He has some end in mind; of that I have no doubt."

"But what?" Turfen asked the question which everyone else was about to voice.

"Ah, . . . there's the problem. I cannot be certain of anything yet."

"But you must have some suspicion if you've given it so much thought."

"Yes, I have."

"Well, come then Rueggan; tell us what you think."

Rueggan took a piece of parchment from a pocket of his tunic and, with it, began to fumble. "I'm not certain you understand . . ."

"By my beard, speak!" exclaimed Turfen. "Tell us what you think!"

"He is planning to take possession of the Obelisk; lay his hands upon The Dom; destroy us and life as we know it."

"Zounds! Surely you must be mistaken!"

The Council Chamber echoed to exclamations of disbelief, followed by raised voices as each Master Wizard attempted to be heard above the rest. Turfen had to bang his wooden gavel several times to restore some semblance of order.

"Do we then rid ourselves of this storm," he asked of Rueggan, "or do we sit back and endure it?"

"We have no choice. We must drive it away."

"And our power?" asked Shepf. "For how long can we continue to pit ourselves against N'Borg before The Dom fades and leaves us entirely undefended?"

"That I don't know," Rueggan admitted. "We must prepare ourselves as best we can and show no signs of weakness to our enemy."

"And hope Groosh and Nimbo have found the Maj-Dron," added Haapf.

"There's always hope, my dears," said Wodema, trying to sound more reassuring than she really felt inside.

After poring over their spellbooks long into the night, The Council of Wizards combined to release a spell of considerable potency through The Dom, which caused the storm to wither away. By the time the wizards sat down to their breakfasts, strong sunlight was slanting through the window-slots of the Obelisk.

It was a glorious morning. A sky of the most flawless blue arched above the Kappah, and the sun flashed off the snows on the higher reaches. Over Keldorran, a diaphanous veil of mist touched softly upon the trees as the cool moisture held by the earth beneath was relinquished to the warming air. Far away to the west, the Rahpans of the Gadazorri left a tracery of lace-patterned wakes as their sails filled with a steady offshore breeze, pushing them lightly over the emerald sea towards the Delta of the River Cauld.

All Krystonia rejoiced in the sun's return and the lands echoed and rang with the noise of those who toiled without rest to restore some semblance of order.

Wodema stood before the Obelisk and turned her face to feel the soft warm touch of the sun. She smiled, fancying she could just hear the sound of the crops growing apace on the flatlands. She shared the hope of many: perhaps the storm had been N'Borg's final attempt to break down their resistance and, having failed, he would now leave them alone.

Though Rueggan, as always, cautioned against premature optimism, he had no desire to suppress the joy of those whose hearts and minds indulged in the fine weather.

Just after midday, two dark specks were sighted in the eastern sky, flying low towards the Krystellate Obelisk; Groosh and Nimbo! Everyone hurried outside to greet them and hear their news from the Cluod-Hakkom. As soon as they landed, the dragons related their tale.

The Maj-Dron had not escaped the awful weather and had experienced many difficulties of their own. Frequent sandstorms of uncommon ferocity had disrupted their progress to such an extent, they had barely reached halfway to Kazm Ori when Groosh and Nimbo spotted their Yurda from the air. After a few fraught moments when the Maj-Dron had suspected the dragons of harbouring similar intent to N'Grall, Shigger had risen from out of the sand to receive their message. The gravity of The Council's plight did not take long to hit home; he briefly consulted with some of his fellows before telling the dragons they would willingly do whatever they could to help. The wizards, he said, could take heart; their Yurda were already laden with many Krystals uncovered by the sandstorms and the dragons could assure them that the Maj-Dron would return with all haste to Tholgah-Loh.

"Wonderful!" Turfen enthused. "We are deeply indebted to you, noble dragons."

"On the contrary," said Groosh; "the debt is ours for, alone among our kind, we have seen the lands beyond the Kappah."

"That we have," agreed Nimbo. "And what stories do we take back to tell the young ones!"

"The thanks of all who support the Great Design goes with you to Cairn Tor," said Turfen. "May I, however, before you leave, request your indulgence in a further matter?"

"Of what nature?" inquired Groosh.

"The Clans of Om-ba-Don must be informed of the Maj-Drons' return to Tholgah-Loh. And Moplos will have to be told to come and collect their supplies."

"Do you credit us only with the sense of birds?" asked Groosh indignantly. "We have spoken with the Om-ba-Don not a day since and have already told them as much. You may expect Moplos with the new dawn."

"I beg your pardons," said Turfen, flushed with embarrassment. "I intended no offence."

"Think nothing of it, Doyen of The Guild. You are not the first, and will hardly be the last, to undervalue the worth of dragons."

Turfen would have cause to remember Nimbo's prophecy in the very near future . . .

The hope which the long day of sunshine had implanted in the minds of the wizards was cruelly shattered the very next morning. Just before dawn, ominous cloud-banks drifted outwards from the Waste of Shugg, obscuring the moons and stars. By the time that Moplos arrived at the Obelisk with two other members of his Clan and several Gowdans, the clouds were unleashing their burdens of iced rain over the Valley of Wendlock. The faces of the Spellcasters were grim and, though few spoke, their thoughts were easily read.

By mid-afternoon the storms had reached the Gadazorri, off the coast. Tulan was up on deck, checking progress when the first drops of rain touched his shoulder and soaked through his tunic's thin fabric. He shivered and, not for the first time, cursed the sky. "Halve the sheet!" he commanded his crew. "Then change out of your tunics before the storm breaks."

The crew quickly carried out his instructions and soon reappeared on deck, clad in heavily greased storm-capes. Already the rain hissed through the rigging and slapped on the deck's wooden planks, before running off into the scuppers.

"I'll go atop and look for a safe place to anchor, eh Captain?" enquired Krellick.

"No. We'll run as we are for now. I want to make the Delta before nightfall."

"I'll signal the others then. Let them know what we're about"

"If you wish; but whatever they decide to do, we'll go on alone if we must!"

During his visit to Sobul, Tulan had wondered at the deserted houses with their doors thrown open to the wind until, approaching the orchards and fruit groves which nestled in the low hills behind the settlement, he had witnessed a scene of utter devastation.

Where orderly rows of trees once stood, their boughs drooping under the weight of swelling fruits, a tangle of contorted branches, trunks and roots poked through a steadily advancing field of mud; an entire hillside behind the orchards had slipped forward and down after constant heavy rain had destabilised the soil. The carefully cultivated fruit crop, which provided Sobul with its livelihood, had been wiped out at a stroke by the unstoppable sea of mud. Only one question remained unanswered; where were all the inhabitants?

In consequence of so depressing a discovery, Tulan and his fellow Captains had promptly decided to set sail for the Shadi-Sampi. Trade was suffering badly because of the storms and they needed to know what, if anything, could be salvaged. They might, it was becoming increasingly likely, have to curtail their regular pattern, put ashore and find the fruit they so urgently needed for themselves.

Running before the wind with sail reefed, the Rahpans made good time, drawing in sight of the sandspit on the west side of the Delta's mouth as the day was drawing to a close. They dropped anchor at a safe distance from the shore and prepared to wait out the night.

The bad weather showed no signs of abating by next morning and, through the lashing rain, grey sea became one with grey sky. With no way of knowing, from where they lay, what conditions were like in the Delta, Tulan decided to go and inspect for himself. He ordered a trading boat to be prepared and was rowed by its crew to the shore. Having beached their craft, the oarsmen followed him as he marched with the wind through coarse wet grass to the sandspit's highest point. From there, with a clear view of the river's mouth, their stomachs turned at what they saw.

A torrent of dirty brown water swept down the channel and out to sea. Much of the spit upon which they stood had already been washed away — the one on the east side must have succumbed for no sign of it remained. No Skeat, nor even a Rahpan, could make headway against a current of such force. Worse, borne upon the flood like strange and sinister beasts whose grotesque limbs embraced the chilling air, was a forest of floating trees.

Tulan's mind was made up. A meeting was called on board his ship of every Captain and First Mate. "As I see it," he said, after reporting the horrors in store beyond the spit, "trade is finished for the year and the sooner we come to terms with it, the better. I suggest we find safe anchorage and then we go ashore. I shall make for the Valley of Wendlock, to find out what has become of the Spell-casters and report the destruction of Sobul. Should anyone wish to accompany me, I will be only too pleased."

Krellick and Salaar were first to volunteer, though soon the mood was unanimous. "But what of our vessels?" inquired Salaar. "Who will stay with them?"

"Two or three old hands to each should suffice," said Tulan, "to protect the females and keep a tight ship."

"In my experience the females run tight ships already," quipped Krellick.

"They do indeed," agreed Tulan, "but these are strange times. I'm sure our minds would be less troubled to know a few useful blades were aboard."

"And fruit?" Salaar asked.

"There's enough in the lockers to see them through till we return. On the way back we can collect enough to last us over winter."

When news of Tulan's proposal reached the crews, there was hardly one amongst them whose heart did not leap at the prospect of a journey into unknown lands. As much as they disliked the feel of solid ground beneath their feet, they had all heard talk of the tower where the wizards worked, which touched against the clouds; now they might see it for themselves. Each Captain had, as a result, to draw lots to determine who should stay.

The next morning, having secured their ships in a nearby sheltered bay, five hundred or more Gadazorri, each armed with a cutlass, went ashore. With Tulan and Tallac at their head, they began the long trek to Wendlock.

Two days after Moplos had departed for Tholgah-Loh, I arrived at the Obelisk to keep my scheduled appointment with Reammon. After a brief exchange concerning some obscure translations which the Librarian had recently acquired, we climbed the spiralling staircase of the Obelisk's central tower. It is as well that Reammon is endowed with plenty of patience, for I needed to pause frequently to catch my breath before we finally emerged beneath The Dom's raised plinth.

I was pleased to discover we were not alone; Shepf, his back towards us, was studying a spellbook lying open at his feet.

"Bother and blast!" he let out, throwing up his hands in flustered dismay.

"Ho, now Shepf! What," I inquired, "puts you in such in a mood?"

"Oh, hello there Kephren old friend," he replied, somewhat surprised to see me. "It's this lousy weather again, I'm afraid. One thing after another, spell after spell. I really am quite exhausted."

"Trying to bring out the sun?"

"No. It's that dratted cloud." He pointed to the north-east where a huge cloud sat brooding over the furthermost edge of the forest. "There's a storm and a half in that one. Just look at it! I can't budge it an inch with my usual spells."

"N'Borg has a hand in it, you think?" asked Reammon.

"Undoubtedly," Shepf replied. "It's moving against the prevailing wind. I'd better inform Turfen and see what he wants me to do."

"Poor Shepf," Reammon said, as soon as he had departed. "He's hardly slept since Reawakening. I sometimes think we're lucky, you and I, not to be involved in magic."

Early next morning, Groosh and Nimbo landed outside the Obelisk and sent an Apprentice within to fetch Turfen. He appeared before them presently, ahead of Rueggan and Shepf.

"We seek your help now, Doyen," said Groosh, clearly in some distress.

"I will do what I can," replied Turfen. "What brings you here so early? Can it be the cloud?"

"Yes," said Groosh, bemused by the wizard's calmness. "It must be shifted immediately!"

"Don't worry," soothed Turfen, "Shepf's preparations are well under way. You may assure Grunch on your return that the storm will be dealt with as soon as Moplos arrives with the Krystals from Tholgah-Loh."

"But it's more than just a storm!" exclaimed Nimbo. "Please help us, Master Wizard," he appealed directly to Shepf.

"I shall, I shall. As soon as Moplos returns from . . ."

"No!" said Groosh, smoke wisping from his snout. "We have already told you it is no ordinary storm. The cloud carries winter within. Already the stones around Cairn Tor grow white with ice and we shiver within our caverns!"

"N'Borg!" rasped Rueggan. "Now I see; he's coming!"

Turfen and Shepf glanced at each other and then at Rueggan, aghast.

"He comes!" Rueggan repeated. "He believes us ready for the taking."

"What are we to do?" asked Shepf.

"We will call The Council to meet in the chamber at once," said Turfen, "Groosh and Nimbo had better go back to Cairn Tor and tell their fellow-dragons to stay deep within their caverns while we do all we can to warm things up."

As Groosh and Nimbo took to the air and flew off towards Cairn Tor, the three wizards re-entered the Obelisk. They had barely crossed the threshold when they were stopped in their tracks by the sound of many raised voices, coming from beyond the encircling trees. Tador appeared moments later, his tunic hoisted above his knees, running towards them as fast as his legs would carry him.

"Doyen!" he shouted. "Come quickly!" The settlements in Wendlock have been attacked!"

"What!?"

"It is true! The inhabitants come by the hundred to seek sanctuary inside The Henge!"

Nothing could have prepared the three wizards for the sight which greeted them as they stared downhill from the trees. Tador had not exaggerated. Hundreds of settlement dwellers poured between the standing stones; and still more were approaching behind them.

"Rueggan, find out who their spokesmen are," bade Turfen, "and bring them with you to the Council Chamber. Will you, Tador, stay here and try to instil some order. Reassure them if you can, but do not let them into the Obelisk. We must not be distracted from our purpose." Turfen was astonished by his own composure. It was as if his mind had detached itself from the rest of his being and was addressing each problem in turn. He just hoped it would remain so.

For once Turfen did not have to call for order before a Council meeting began. As he took his seat at the table, only a few subdued whispers were exchanged before silence descended completely.

"You will all be aware of recent events," he began, "so I shall waste no time elaborating further. I have called this meeting so that we may decide how best to resist the attack which will surely come from N'Borg. It seems he plans to take the Obelisk by both magic and brute force. We are all acquainted by now with the weight of his spell-making and, whilst The Dom remains in our possession and continues to lend strength to our words, we can at least be his equal. Yet we still do not know how many bear arms in his name. From what the Bobolls tell us, and from the boldness of his thrust, they must be many indeed. This is where our greatest weakness lies. We wizards have scant knowledge of physical fighting and few weapons with which to confront him."

"What about those who have fled the settlements?" asked Haapf. "Will they not fight with us?"

"I expect they will. But don't forget they were driven from their lands by forces too powerful for them to withstand!"

"What news have they?" asked Rohan.

"You shall hear it for yourselves," replied Turfen. "Would you ask the spokesmen to enter now, please Rueggan?"

The spokesmen filed into the chamber as Rueggan held open the door, and stood in line before The Council.

"I bid you all welcome," said Turfen, "though I wish you were here under happier circumstances. I see you are weary and bear many wounds. The wizardess Wodema will attend to them soon, but first we would ask what fate has befallen you and your peoples."

"Hogfaces!" boomed one whose wounded head had been roughly dressed with strips of fabric. "Loads of 'em with axes laid into us without warning!"

"Some were much bigger with spikes on the end of long poles," remarked another.

"We made 'em fight," said a third, "but they caught us on the hop. Anyways, it was useless. You knock one down and there's suddenly ten more in his place!"

"So they are many in number?" asked Wodema, containing an urge to start treating their cuts and bruises.

"You bet they are, lady, swarms of 'em," said Headwound. His colleagues nodded emphatically in agreement.

"How many are you?" asked Rueggan.

"A lot less than we were this mornin', that's for sure," replied Headwound. "But enough to give a good account of ourselves, now we're all together."

"You have many weapons?" enquired Turfen hopefully.

"Few axes, the odd blade and my brother's got a spear. Shovels and picks are just as good if you know how to use them; not to mention staffs and our bare hands . . ."

Though their catalogue of arms did not inspire in him much confidence, Turfen admired their resilience. If they represented the mood of their peoples, the wizards had steadfast allies indeed. "You will fight for us then, I take it?" he asked.

"No choice, Mister Doyen," said Headwound. "We've nowhere else to go, now that our homes have been overrun!"

"And you are all from Wendlock?"

"I'm not," said a voice from the back. "I am Phillian, Fugleman of Sobul."

"What? Has Sobul been attacked?" asked Rueggan incredulously.

"Not in the sense you mean. We came to seek help of a different kind. Our orchards have all been destroyed by a mudslide and we need replacement stock."

"We can certainly help you," said Rohan, "if we ever get the chance!"

"Don't worry," said Turfen. "We will! But now let's concern ourselves with the matter of our defence."

"We can build a barricade," responded one of the spokesmen.

"Good idea," approved Rueggan, glad to hear that someone else relied on practical solutions to problems.

"And the Trolles are building a bridge," observed another. "Though I'm not sure what good it will do where it is."

"The Trolles are here?" asked Rueggan.

"Yes. Came out of Keldorran just after we arrived."

"Splendid!" said Rueggan. "I must go and see them right away."

"When you've done that," suggested Turfen, "will you and our friends from the settlements take charge of our outer defences? We Spell-casters can then serve the cause by concentrating our minds on the magic."

"Suits us," chorused the spokesmen.

"And me," agreed Rueggan.

"I want to see all Master Wizards at the top of the Obelisk with their spellbooks, concluded Turfen. "Let's go to work; and good luck to the Great Design!"

When Groosh and Nimbo returned to Cairn Tor, they found it completely engulfed in the cloud, apart from the very tips of its peaks. They searched in vain for a way through the swirling fog, whose biting cold threatened to cool their blood and render them incapable of flight. They could hardly bring themselves to consider what conditions were like inside the caverns, deciding instead to return to the Obelisk and demand that the wizards get rid of the cloud forthwith.

Barely had they begun when a fireball flashed over Groosh's head, upon which he twisted instinctively and plunged into a crash dive. Hearing Nimbo cry out in pain, he looked about him only to see his unfortunate brood-brother fall from the sky, the life gone from him before his body was dashed upon the rocks.

Still Groosh dropped like a stone, another fireball passing so close he felt the sudden pulse of its heat across his tender flanks. When it seemed certain that he too was doomed to die upon the rocks, he opened his wings, levelled out and rocketed skywards, climbing higher and higher till sure his assailant could no way have kept him in range.

The Henchdragon emerged from the cloud on cue, heading directly towards him. The air exploded in a confusion of orange and vermillion as both dragons unleashed searing bolts of flame; they missed. Swooping and soaring, veering and looping in a bid to outwing each

N'Borg in the throne room of The Krak, plotting against Krystonia.

other, they streaked the sky with their vapour trails, and scorched the ground beneath them with the heat of their breath.

But the contest was unequal from the start. Groosh, for all his fleetness of wing, could not take refuge in the cloud, nor match the Henchdragon's firepower. Each time Groosh launched an attack, N'Grall would dart into the cloud and reappear elsewhere in the sky, forcing his foe to use every trick he knew to avert being roasted alive.

Not yet fully recovered from his arduous journey to the Cluod-Hakkom, Groosh began to tire first. Knowing full well it was only a matter of time before he succumbed, he waited until his opponent vanished again in the cloud and banking sharply, swooped beneath the canopy of Keldorran's trees.

"Hide while you still have somewhere to hide!" roared N'Grall. His voice was cold and cruel. "I will not waste my fire on such a miserable opponent as you when there are better to be fried close by!"

Groosh was so incensed, he was tempted to take to the air and resume their duel; but his wings were heavy, his furnace near extinguished. Seeing wisdom in saving his strength, he vowed to avenge Nimbo's death if it was the last thing he ever did.

Under Rueggan's direction, the environs of the Obelisk took on the air of a fortress and much was accomplished in a short span of time. Just beyond the standing stones, a semi-circular trench had been excavated by the settlement dwellers and an embankment of earth raised behind. The Trolles had finished constructing their bridge and, to their disconcertion, had been ordered by the inventor-wizard to saw it in two parts, across the upper beams. Mounted on wheels from a pair of battered old wagons, the half-bridges were hauled up the hill until Rueggan was satisfied with their placement. Consulting outlines upon a scrap of parchment, he supervised their adaptation into contraptions for a purpose known only to himself. The Trolles then felled a mature tree, much to Rohan's dismay, from the ring surrounding the Obelisk. They cut it and shaped, hammered and drilled under the watchful eye of Groc who stood in their midst and barked unintelligible orders, waving his arms and growing ever more pale as sawdust rained down upon him.

Headwound, meanwhile, had overseen the building of a barricade from carts and the plentiful brushwood dislodged in the recent high winds. Not intended as a last line of defence but more as an obstruction, it was capable of being hauled uphill in an ever-tightening noose, finally to be incorporated within the circle of trees as an unbroken wall before the Obelisk.

As the Trolles' task neared completion, Rueggan gave some of them new jobs. One group he despatched to Wendlock's head to gather large boulders from the broken ground thereabouts and deliver them back with all haste. The other he assigned to chop logs and carry them to the top of the hill. Then he addressed the knot of Gorphs who, till then, had been dogging his footsteps. "Fetch it, I tell you!" he growled after brief explanation. "Don't hang about; go on!"

Huddled together, some clutching each other tightly, the Gorphs began to whimper.

"Enough of that!" Rueggan insisted. "Do as I say; and look sharp!"

Hand in hand, the little creatures obediently filed out of the Henge and headed for the Valley. Rueggan, his face betraying his real concern for their welfare, watched them until they had vanished from sight before directing his attentions back to the industrious Trolles.

"Here they come!" bellowed a lookout Apprentice, gesticulating wildly with outstretched arms.

"Curses!" muttered Rueggan. "They're attacking from the wrong direction. "Take up your positions!" he yelled, hands cupped to his mouth.

His order was echoed along the line of spokesmen and, at once, the displaced inhabitants picked up their shovels, hoes, picks and anything else which would serve as a weapon and hurried to their designated posts.

Then, to everyone else's surprise, Phillian, Fugleman of Sobul, ran out from behind the barricade, his people hot on his heels. "Gadazorri!" they hailed. "Gadazorri!"

Rueggan heard their cry but thought his ears were deceiving him. Only when he recognised Tulan and Tallac at the edge of the broad swathe of open ground, was he finally convinced.

"By my beard!" he exclaimed, slapping Headwound on the back. "We grow stronger, my friend!"

The Gadazorri were as relieved to see Rueggan as he was to see them. Their blades were already bloodied and many of their tunics torn.

"We feared The Council must be deposed," said Tulan, "for the Pigmen are everywhere beyond here."

"You mean Hogfaces," said Headwound.

"No, you both mean Snords," corrected Rueggan.

"By whatever names they are known, we fought with them not long since."

"Have you lost many of your company?"

"A few will not be returning to the sea," sighed Tulan, "but we lost far fewer than they. One Gadazorri is the equal of three Pigmen."

"It may not be enough," observed Headwound. "Listen!"

From within the cloud steadily advancing over the plains between Keldorran and The Henge, could be heard the marching ranks of Snords and Honji which had plundered the settlements earlier in the day.

"Prepare the catapults!" yelled Rueggan.

The Trolles were extremely proud of their latest handiwork and let no one else assist them with loading the slings or priming the firing mechanisms. Groc, revelling in the chance to assert his authority, strolled around the structures, tapping a peg here, testing a joint there until, satisfied that all was in good working order, he signalled to Rueggan. The Gadazorri, meanwhile, moved down the hill and stood behind the embankment, shoulder to shoulder with their friends from Sobul. There they drew their blades.

"Now it's up to them," mused Rueggan. "All we can do is wait."

From the fringe of the cloud, several Honji presently appeared, bearing a shared heavy burden towards the Henge. As they drew near, it proved to be a small platform, upon which a dark figure was plainly seated.

"Come no closer," Rueggan bellowed when the Honji were well within earshot, "if you value your skins!"

The Honji stopped in their tracks and set the platform onto the ground. The sinister figure stepped down and came forward alone. It was, Rueggan recognised instantly, none other than N'Chakk!

"State your business!" challenged Rueggan.

"Greetings, oh wizard without power and maker of playthings," N'Chakk sneered. "I bring you the words of the Great One."

"Ha!" scoffed Rueggan. "Some Great One who entrusts his words to his pet potion-maker!"

N'Chakk was visibly angered by Rueggan's insult and by the laughter it provoked amongst the settlement dwellers.

"The words of a fool will make fools laugh," he retorted. "It seems that I, Master of the Dark Art, must converse with the Master of All Fools!"

"Fools we may be," answered Rueggan, "but we know no Master here."

"But soon you shall," N'Chakk hissed venomously. "The

Great One commands you to lay down your arms in submission."

"Go back and tell him we cannot comply," snapped Rueggan, "for, as you can see, our arms are fixed to our bodies and, no matter who commands it, they will not come undone!"

His affrontery was more than N'Chakk could bear. "You will soon be parted from your heads!" he threatened with malice. "Before the day is out you will serve N'Borg or perish!"

"Be off with you; and tell the Ugly One not to waste any more of our time!" spat Rueggan, bending down to pull up a clod of earth. "Here!" he said, throwing it over the embankment. "Give him this with our compliments and tell him he'll get no more from us!"

N'Chakk glowered wickedly and retraced his steps to the platform with the jibes of the settlement dwellers ringing in his ears. "Remind me," he invited his escort while climbing into his seat, "to give treble rations to the one who brings me the head of that arrogant maker of toys!"

Moments after N'Chakk's withdrawal, the cloud became suffused with a cold blue light which grew brighter and brighter until, with a crack that rended the sky, a fork of lightning flashed through the air and smote the Obelisk's white tower.

"Now!" cried Turfen.

Members of The Council of Wizards, hands linked to form an unbroken chain round The Dom, began to chant in unison, their eyes closed, every fibre of their beings concentrated upon a single incantation. In answer to their words, the orb of white light burning constantly at The Dom's core, expanded and grew in intensity. To those below, the top of the Obelisk seemed enveloped in a sphere of radiance brighter than the midday sun.

A second stroke of blue lightning was discharged by the

cloud, to be countered from the Obelisk by a bolt of sheer white light. Where they touched, an explosion of sparks showered down from the sky, to flicker and die before touching the ground.

The air between Keldorran and the Krystellate Obelisk reverberated to a profusion of pulses as spells hurled from one side were parried by the other. Having searched for a weakness and so far, found none, N'Borg intensified his attacks upon the Obelisk. The Council retaliated by focusing their power on the cloud. The magical forces of Light and Darkness were locked in a far-reaching duel; the battle for spell supremacy had begun. Failure of nerve on either side would mean unqualified defeat.

The sound of many drums signalled the advance of N'Borg's armed forces upon the Henge. Lines of Snords flanked by Honji marched out from beneath the trees at Keldorran's edge, in time to the drums' insistant beat. From under the cloud, a wall of Honji appeared, their pikes thrust forward intently. No sooner had they emerged than so did more Legions of Snords — so many were they in number, it seemed as though a river of lava was flowing from the cloud and nothing could prevent it engulfing the Henge.

It was then Rueggan realised how small a force he led. The embankment and barricade, which he had been depending upon to withstand any attack, appeared to shrink before his eyes. At best they might slow the advance; no way would they stop it. The Great Design seemed doomed against such devilish opposition.

Rueggan was about to leave the barricade and join the Gadazorri behind the embankment when the drums fell silent; the invading army had stopped in its tracks. No longer were its rank and file facing onto the Henge; they looked and pointed in some disarray towards the Kappah. When he followed their gaze, Rueggan let out a heartfelt sigh of relief.

Clad in the armour of their forbears, their Cladya axes and their spiked Hahton shields held before them, the massed Clans of Om-ba-Don had descended the foothills and were fast approaching the Henge. At their feet, small flecks of white flashed on an off like welcoming signals of light.

"The Om-ba-Don! The Bobolls!" cried Rueggan, hardly able to believe his eyes. "Now we'll show them how to fight!"

Hope returned to the Henge of Oria as the Om-ba-Don took up positions beyond the embankment and turned, spiked shields outermost, to face the Snords. Taking hold of the Gowdan's halters, the Bobolls led the heavy-laden pack-animals over the defensive earthwork and inside the Henge, where the inventor wizard greeted them eagerly.

"Glad we weren't too late," said Poffles. "I believe you wanted some Krystal?"

"You've brought Krystal?"

"Some," replied Trumph, indicating Mos's panniers. "It's in those baskets. Shall we unload them now?"

"Yes," urged Rueggan, "but not here. Get your friends together and take them up to the top of the Obelisk. Then stack the Krystals around The Dom. Whatever happens, you are not to speak or even whisper. Under no circumstances must you break the Council's concentration. Understood?"

Accused of treasonable behaviour by their leader, N'Tormet, the Honji were shamed into action. Poking and prodding the snivelling Snords, they soon restored order in their ranks. The advance resumed to the beating of the drums.

As the first wave of Snords charged headlong into war, the eerie sounds of the raging spell-storm were quickly subdued by the clash and clang of metal on metal. The Om-ba-Dons' defensive wall stood firm, those to the front dropping down on one knee and presenting the full face of their shields, as those behind wielded their axes, slaying Snords by the score.

The Honji thrust forward as the Snords fell back to regroup. Aiming over the long line of shields, they stayed well clear of the axe-swingers' reach while attempting to impale them on the ends of their pikes. They met with some success without achieving their objective and breaching the wall.

Again the Snords charged into the fray, but the Clans took a terrible toll and the bodies of their dead piled up in front of the shields.

So many were the followers of N'Borg, such losses made little impression on the ranks of expendable Snords. Yet N'Tormet sensed wisdom in new tactics and directed two fresh Legions to pour in from the flanks. Forced to take evasive measures, the Clans' resources were stretched too thinly. Slowly but surely, they were being overrun.

Rueggan could see what was happening. In mean mood he hurried down to Gadazorri and the people of Sobul, divided them swiftly into two equal groups and launched a bold counter-offensive, deploying them left and right. Over the embankment they ran to supplement the axes of the Om-ba-Don at the margins of their battered wall.

Confronted head-on by a Snord, Rueggan suddenly realised he was completely unarmed. Luck was with him for, as the Snord prepared to strike, old Tallac's blade hit home. The Snord squealed and fell dead at Rueggan's feet.

Thankful for the additions to their front the Om-ba-Don spread forward with their shields to the fore, knocking aside Snords by the dozen with each wide sweep of their huge arms and leaving the Gadazorri to finish them off. Just when it seemed that the defenders of the Henge were gaining the upper hand, N'Grall swooped down from the cloud.

N'Grall cared not if his flames burned friend or foe; their lives were of no consequence against the power which he would command when N'Borg held sway in the Obelisk. He flew low above the many Snords still waiting to enter the strife and began to rain fireballs down upon the seething field of blood.

The Om-ba-Don, who had stood firm for so long against the massed forces of N'Borg, had no answer to this unexpected onslaught from the air. All order was lost as they held up their shields to ward of N'Grall's searing flames. Snords and Honji surged forward through their erstwhile impenetrable wall.

N'Grall flew inside the Henge and, with intense satisfaction, set fire to the barricade. Instantly, Bobolls settlement dwellers, Spell-casters and Trolles retreated uphill towards the Obelisk. N'Grall picked some of them off, whilst the remainder entered the ring of trees. Unable to pursue them, for the magic inside the trees was still too strong, he turned his cruel attentions back upon the belligerents.

Inside the circle of trees, Headwound had formed an idea. After a heated discussion with Groc commandeering one of the catapults, several settlement dwellers helped him manoeuvre the machine into position and, unbeknown to N'Grall, he took careful aim.

The first boulder overshot its intended target but, none the less, it flattened three Honji. The second fell short embedding itself in the embankment. The third, unleashed by the Trolles who had only just discovered the true function of their catapults, hit the Henchdragon hard on the nape of his neck and knocked him out. He fell in a heap in the midst of the Snords, who regarded his undignified form with disrespect and, in truth, they hoped he was dead.

But N'Grall had succeeded in blighting the hopes of the Obelisk's defenders. Though his downfall had allowed those taking refuge within the trees to charge down the hill and aid their allies, their efforts lacked co-ordination. Small groups fought independently, falling one by one in the face of overwhelming odds. Pockets of Om-ba-Don, isolated from the main body of the Clans, laid into the enemy swarming around their legs, till pulled down and swallowed up by the advancing hordes. Bobolls 'zumped' in and out of flailing limbs, biting legs, chewing fingers and pulling hair until, exhausted, they fell asleep and were trampled underfoot. Slowly, the forces of the Henge were pushed back behind the embankment, higher and higher up the hill.

From a safe distance, N'Chakk was greatly relieved to see the Snords at last make significant inroads. He had watched his Master flinch a little earlier as he struggled to keep his concentration, and had guessed that The Council had somehow increased the output of their power. No matter; if N'Borg could withstand them for just a while longer, the Obelisk was bound to fall and all their spell-making would count for nought. Looking up, he perceived that the cloud was thinning; N'Borg's own power was beginning to wane. He raised a heavy sack to his shoulders, full of Krystals which he'd intended to keep for himself; but the needs of N'Borg would have to come first. After all, it was a long walk back to Malforan!

The Gorphs sent to Wendlock by Rueggan before the fighting commenced, had since returned with a sack of their own. But this one contained no Krystal; whatever was within wriggled so strenuously that they had to let go of it several times. So loud were its howls of protest that, when the Gorphs tried to sneak inside the Henge, they attracted N'Tormet's attention. He promptly ordered two Honji to capture them and their sack, his stomach rumbling at the thought that it must contain food.

The Gorphs were ushered before him at pike-point. Smiling wickedly, he poked one of them in the belly and licked his lips on feeling plentiful meat. But the writhing contents of the sack intrigued him even more; he ordered the Gorphs to untie it at once. They shook their heads emphatically and, even when the Honji prodded them with their pikes, they still refused to oblige.

N'Tormet was outraged. Never before had he encountered such insubordination and open defiance of his will. Swearing to stew the bite-sized beasts in short order, he commanded the Honji to open the sack.

The moment the sack fell away, the Gorphs took off at speed. Despatching the Honji to retrieve them, N'Tormet surveyed his prize; whatever it was did not look particularly appetising. None the less, he bent down and reached out a finger . . .

The chasing Honji froze in mid-stride when they heard their General's cry of pain. Glancing back, they saw him running away, faster than they knew that he could, with a strange cuboid creature hot on his heels. If N'Tormet had heard them cheering, he would no doubt have boiled them alive, along with the Gorphs.

Gwillum knew precisely how many days he had spent cooped up in that awful dungeon before managing to outwit his guards and escape. Eight! Eight whole days without food! The belt around his waist had been tightened by eight notches — that was how he knew.

Rohan would be hopping mad but, for once, Gwillum had the comfort of a good excuse. Even if the wizard did not readily accept his story about being captured by Snords and cast into the dungeon, he would be forced to admit that something awful must have befallen his Apprentice when he saw how much weight he had lost. And what's more he had found a Krystal. That should go some way to redeeming himself when he saw Rohan again . . . If he saw Rohan again!

Gwillum was tired lost, confused and ravenously hungry. If he could find somewhere dry and warm to rest, he would take a short nap and dream about a table piled high with food. Dreaming about food, he had found was the next best thing to eating — though it rarely appeased the appetite, it never resulted in indigestion.

He came upon a dragon, apparently fast asleep, and almost sneaked off without introducing himself. Dragons, Gwillum believed, looked quite threatening at close quarters. But then, his fear of dragons overcome by enticing visions of home and food, he perceived an opportunity to return quickly to the Obelisk without the need to expend any more of his own flagging energy.

"Excuse me dragon," he grandly proclaimed, "I am Gwillum, Master Wizard and a member of The Council. I demand you take me back to the Obelisk, right now!" As an afterthought he added, "And should you happen to have any food, I insist you hand it over!"

Once he had recovered from the shock of seeing Gwillum before him, Groosh struggled wearily to his feet. "Tell me, my fat little Apprentice wizard and Master Liar; how long have you been out of circulation?"

"Please!" Gwillum begged, dropping his masquerade. "Take me home; I'm starving. Look!" He showed his belt to Groosh.

"By my breath!" snorted Groosh. "The Obelisk is under attack and he thinks only of his stomach! What sort of Apprentices do they train these days?"

"Under attack? What are you on about, dragon?" He looked at Groosh circumspectly. "you're not . . . you know . . . err . . . an unstable sort, are you?"

Groosh, tired though he was, had to laugh. "No; You are quite safe in my company."

Gwillum was visibly relieved. "In that case you won't mind taking me back to the Obelisk."

To his credit, Groosh managed to keep his patience and explained recent events to Gwillum. The Apprentice grew paler as the dragon recounted more and more.

"And you can't fly because you're cold?"

"That is so," sighed Groosh.

"Then I shall make you warm again and, together we will liberate my friends."

"Even if you could make me warm, which I doubt, we cannot hope to help them by ourselves. It would take all the dragons of Cairn Tor to do that."

"Then we'll go and get them first!" Gwillum cursed his luck at having found such an apathetic dragon. "I have a Krystal!" he proclaimed, holding it out so that Groosh could see. "I can make you and all the other dragons warm with this," he said with confidence.

"If you can make me fly," said Groosh hopefully, "then we will do as you say."

"Right!" said Gwillum. "Shut your eyes and keep them shut!"

"Dear-Oh-Dear!" Groosh moaned, "He sounds like Stoope!"

"Keep them shut!" bade Gwillum, relishing the prospect of a spot of unauthorised spell-making. "Now let me see . . . Morrhobbur . . . Thorhobbur . . . or was it Longhobbur first? . . . err . . ."

"Come on! Hurry up!" Groosh complained. "You can either do it or you can't."

"Hang on. You're interrupting my magical flow. Longhobbur, Morrhobbur, Thorhobbur, Gan. Sang-holloh, Ding-holloh, ZAN!!"

The Krystal burst into life, radiating with fired-light which touched upon the dragon's body and made Gwillum feel quite lively.

"There. How's that?"

"Well," said Groosh "I'd never have believed it! You're pretty good for an Apprentice. I take back all I said!" He stretched his wings and beat them vigorously, well pleased.

"Thank me later when I am seated in front of a table of

food," replied Gwillum. "Now let's go and release your friends before the Krystal is spent."

The valiant Om-ba-Don were stationed between the trees at the top of the hill, trying to plug the gaps through which Snords were pouring in droves. Bodies littering the hillside and the grass was stained bright crimson, where the blood of Snords and Honji mixed with that of their fallen comrades.

Though the defenders of the Great Design had suffered far fewer casualties than had the forces of N'Borg, their numbers had been significantly less to begin with, and each loss had been harder to bear. They would fight on to the bitter end but the battle, they knew, was lost. Enough Snords were already breaking through to mount a direct assault upon the Obelisk.

And then, from out of the heavens, came the winged dragons of Cairn Tor. Groosh, Orzeven and Spyke were first to sweep down and blow their fired breath into the main body of the Snords, closely followed by second and third flights. The effect was instantaneous; it turned the tide of the battle. To the Snords, the sky seemed full of terrible demons; to their friends, they appeared as avenging spirits.

Those Snords still pushing towards the top of the hill, turned and fled in panic. Those outside the Obelisk, now starved of reinforcements, fought on until they fell.

Sickened by the turn of events, N'Grall would have attacked his former associates, had not the blow he had sustained dented both his armour and his pride. Besides, he knew that Groosh would have long since informed the others about his slaying of Nimbo and, should they once surround him, not even he could escape from them all. He would collect his Master and return to the safety of the Krak. They had come close this time. Next time they would succeed with a vengeance.

But N'Borg had no intention of giving up so easily. Still locked into a fiery battle with The Council, the Evil Lord meant to fight to the end, and no amount of pleading by N'Grall could break his concentration.

The cloud which had protected him from the warmth he so loathed had long since withered away. Yet still he stood firm and unrelenting, his face a contorted mask of unadulterated hate, defying all that the Obelisk had come to represent.

"Quickly, N'Grall!" demanded N'Chakk, who had suddenly appeared from hiding. "Let me ride upon your back, straight and true to the Krak."

"I suffer the weight of none upon my back," the hench dragon snarled.

"Don't be an idiot!" screeched N'Chakk, shaking like a leaf. "Come, take me to the Krak and I will give you anything you ask."

"By what power?"

"Don't you see? He is finished. I, N'Chakk, am the Master now. I command you to take me away!"

"You are no more worthy than those useless runts who run from the enemy. You walk."

"I command! . . ."

N'Grall towered over N'Chakk and, in a threatening whisper which singed the spell-caster's beard, he hissed: "You walk!"

N'Chakk made off in lone haste towards the Forest of Keldorran, determined that, when he was Master of the Krak, he would make the Henchdragon crawl and squirm before him.

N'Grall regarded his Master with sad affection. The dragons of Cairn Tor would be sure to spot him soon, but still he showed no signs of disengaging. N'Grall admired him more for that; it was a laudable quality but, in this case, it was senseless and would achieve nothing. Taking to the air, he wheeled sharply and swooping low, plucked N'Borg from the ground in his talons.

Lying in wait for the fleeing Snords beneath the treetops of Keldorran, the Grumblypeg dragons heard a voice cry out overhead, "No! No! I almost had them! Put me down, you great lump! Put me down!"

Wounds of the flesh heal quickly. Wounds of the heart take longer and, as often as not, they never really heal at all but are merely suffered in silence. Wounds of both kinds were inflicted that day. As the Obelisk's forces rejoiced at the dragons' arrival and began to celebrate victory, they looked about them for old friends with whom to share thanksgiving. Some they found unscathed, oh lucky few; but many more lay dead or dying upon the field of battle.

Tallac was lying beneath the bodies of two Snords when Tulan found him, his tunic was soaked with blood and his breathing short and laboured. He opened his eyes when Tulan raised his head and cradled it in his lap.

"Ah, my son, you are safe." He smiled weakly and closed his eyes again.

"And so are you, my father."

"Oh, yes. I am safe now. I hear the sea."

"No father, not yet. It will be some time before you are well enough to travel back to the sea. You must remain here until you are recovered."

"I hear the sea Tulan, believe me. I hear it now," he said softly.

"But father . . ."

"My waves are breaking upon another shore. My boat lies at anchor and soon . . . soon I will begin another voyage . . ."

The candle burns low. Outside, the wind drives the snow down from the Mountains of Kappah, through the Forest of Keldorran and into the Valley of Wendlock. My eyes grow weary. I shall lay down my quill, throw another log upon the fire and go to sleep. Tomorrow is another day and who knows what it will bring?

As Tallac said, ". . . soon I will begin another voyage . . ."